"You'll have ample opportunity to convince me to sleep with you."

A shock blasted through him as potent as if he'd grabbed a live wire with both hands. "You call that a wager?" He had no idea where he found the strength to joke. "I call it shooting ducks in a barrel."

"Don't you mean fish?" Her dry smile warned him winning wasn't going to be easy. "Getting me to sleep with you isn't the wager. Though I'll admit the thought of you and me has crossed my mind once or twice."

Shane wondered why he wasn't feeling more triumphant at the moment. "Damn, woman. You sure do know how to stroke a man's ego."

"Oh please," she said. "You love playing games. I thought this would appeal to everything you stand for."

"And what is that exactly?"

"You get me to fall for you and I sell you the ranch for ten million."

He hadn't prepared himself properly for the devastation of that other shoe. It was a doozy. "And what needs to happen for you to win?"

"Simple." Her smile was pure evil. "I get you to fall for me."

* * *

Two-Week Texas Seduction is part of the series Texas Cattleman's Club: Blackmail—
No secret—or heart—is safe in Royal, Texas...

Dear Readers,

I'm excited to be participating in my third Texas Cattleman's Club series with *Two-Week Texas Seduction*. Almost from the start I knew Brandee and Shane were going to be a blast to write. From their sexy banter to the slow disintegration of their guards, every moment I spent with them was a joy. This blackmail series is going to be such fun to read. I hope you enjoy Brandee and Shane's story.

All the best,

Cat Schield

CAT SCHIELD

TWO-WEEK TEXAS SEDUCTION

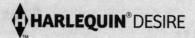

Special thanks and acknowledgment are given
to Cat Schield for her contribution to the Texas
Cattleman's Club: Blackmail miniseries.

Recycling programs
for this product may
not exist in your area.

ISBN-13: 978-0-373-83825-7

Two-Week Texas Seduction

HARLEQUIN®
™ www.Harlequin.com

Printed in U.S.A.

Cat Schield has been reading and writing romance since high school. Although she graduated from college with a BA in business, her idea of a perfect career was writing books for Harlequin. And now, after winning the Romance Writers of America 2010 Golden Heart® Award for Best Contemporary Series Romance, that dream has come true. Cat lives in Minnesota with her daughter, Emily, and their Burmese cat. When she's not writing sexy, romantic stories for Harlequin Desire, she can be found sailing with friends on the St. Croix River, or in more exotic locales, like the Caribbean and Europe. She loves to hear from readers. Find her at catschield.com and follow her on Twitter, @catschield.

Books by Cat Schield

Harlequin Desire

The Black Sheep's Secret Child
Nanny Makes Three

The Sherdana Royals

Royal Heirs Required
A Royal Baby Surprise
Secret Child, Royal Scandal

Las Vegas Nights

At Odds with the Heiress
A Merger by Marriage
A Taste of Temptation

Texas Cattleman's Club: Blackmail

Two-Week Texas Seduction

Visit her Author Profile page at Harlequin.com,
or catschield.com, for more titles!

For everyone trying to make ends meet while keeping your dreams alive. Never give up, never surrender.

One

Before she'd moved to Royal, Texas, few people had ever done Brandee Lawless any favors. If this had left her with an attitude of "you're damned right I can," she wasn't going to apologize. She spoke her mind and sometimes that ruffled feathers. Lately those feathers belonged to a trio of women new to the Texas Cattleman's Club. Cecelia Morgan, Simone Parker and Naomi Price had begun making waves as soon as they'd been accepted as members and Brandee had opposed them at every turn.

Her long legs made short work of the clubhouse foyer and the hallway leading to the high-ceilinged dining room where she and her best friend, Chelsea Hunt, were having lunch. At five feet five inches, she wasn't exactly an imposing figure, but she knew how to make an entrance.

Instead of her usual denim, boots, work shirt and cowboy hat, Brandee wore a gray fit-and-flare sweater dress with lace inset cuffs over a layered tulle slip, also in gray. She'd braided sections of her long blond hair and fastened them with rhinestone-encrusted bobby pins. She noted three pair of eyes watching her progress across the room and imagined the women assessing her outfit. To let them know she wasn't the least bit bothered, Brandee made sure she took her time winding through the diners on her way to the table by the window.

Chelsea looked up from the menu as she neared. Her green eyes widened. "Wow, you look great."

Delighted by her friend's approval, Brandee smiled. "Part of the new collection." In addition to running one of the most profitable ranches in Royal, Texas, Brandee still designed a few pieces of clothing and accessories for the fashion company she'd started twelve years earlier. "What do you think of the boots?"

"I'm sick with jealousy." Chelsea eyed the bright purple Tres Outlaws and grinned. "You are going to let me borrow them, I hope."

"Of course."

Brandee sat down, basking in feminine satisfaction. With all the hours she put in working her ranch, most saw her as a tomboy. Despite a closet full of frivolous, girlie clothes, getting dressed up for the sole purpose of coming into town for a leisurely lunch was a rare occurrence. But this was a celebration. Her first month-long teenage outreach session was booked solid. This summer Hope Springs Camp was going to make a difference in those kids' lives.

"You made quite an impression on the terrible trio." Chelsea tipped her head to indicate the three newly minted members of the Texas Cattleman's Club. "They're staring at us and whispering."

"No doubt hating on what I'm wearing. I don't know why they think I care what they say about me."

It was a bit like being in high school, where the pretty, popular girls ganged up on anyone they viewed as easy prey. Not that Brandee was weak. In fact, her standing in the club and in the community was strong.

"It's pack mentality," Brandee continued. "On their own they feel powerless, but put them in a group and they'll tear you apart."

"I suppose it doesn't help that you're more successful than they are."

"Or that I've been blocking their attempts to run this club like their personal playground. All this politicking is such a distraction. I'd much rather spend my time holed up at Hope Springs, working the ranch."

"I'm sure they'd prefer that, as well. Especially when you show up looking like this." Chelsea gestured to Brandee's outfit. "You look like a million bucks. They must hate it."

"Except I'm wearing a very affordable line of clothing. I started the company with the idea that I wanted the price points to be within reach of teenagers and women who couldn't afford to pay the designer prices."

"I think it's more the way you wear your success.

You are confident without ever having to build yourself up or tear someone else down."

"It comes from accepting my flaws."

"You have flaws?"

Brandee felt a rush of affection for her best friend. An ex-hacker and present CTO of the Hunt & Co. chain of steak houses, Chelsea was the complete package of brains and beauty. From the moment they'd met, Brandee had loved her friend's kick-ass attitude.

"Everyone has things about themselves they don't like," Brandee said. "My lips are too thin and my ears stick out. My dad used to say they were good for keeping my hat from going too low and covering my eyes."

As always, bringing up her father gave Brandee a bittersweet pang. Until she'd lost him to a freak accident when she was twelve, he'd been her world. From him she'd learned how to run a ranch, and the joys of hard work and a job well done. Without his voice in her head, she never would've had the courage to run from the bad situation with her mother at seventeen and to become a successful rancher.

"But you modeled your own designs for your online store," Chelsea exclaimed. "How did you do that if you were so uncomfortable about how you looked?"

"I think what makes us stand out is what makes us interesting. And memorable. Think of all those gorgeous beauty queens competing in pageants. The ones you remember are those who do something wrong and get called out or who overcome disabilities to compete."

"So the three over there are forgettable?" With a

minute twitch of her head, Chelsea indicated the trio of mean girls.

"As far as I'm concerned." Brandee smiled. "And I think they know it. Which is why they work so hard to be noticed."

She'd barely finished speaking when a stir in the air raised her hackles. A second later a tall, athletically built man appeared beside their table, blocking their view of the three women. Shane Delgado. Brandee had detected his ruggedly masculine aftershave a second before she saw him.

"Hey, Shane." Chelsea's earlier tension melted away beneath the mega wattage of Shane's charismatic white grin. Brandee resisted the urge to roll her eyes. Shane would love seeing proof that he'd gotten to her.

"Good to see you, Chelsea." His smooth Texas drawl had a trace of New England in it. "Hello, Brandee."

She greeted him without looking in his direction. "Delgado." She kept her tone neutral and disinterested, masking the way her body went on full alert in his presence.

"You're looking particularly gorgeous today."

Across from her, Chelsea glanced with eyebrows raised from Shane to Brandee and back.

"You're not so bad yourself." She didn't need to check out his long legs in immaculate denim jeans or the crisp tan shirt that emphasized his broad shoulders to know the man looked like a million bucks. "Something I can do for you, Delgado?" She hated that she was playing into his hands by asking, but he wouldn't move on until he'd had his say.

"Do?" He caressed the word with his silver tongue and almost made Brandee shiver.

She recognized her mistake, but the damage was done. Her tone grew impatient as she clarified, "Did you just stop by to say hello or is there something else on your mind?"

"You know what's on my mind." With another man this might have been a horrible pickup line, but Shane had elevated flirting to an art form.

Brandee glanced up and rammed her gaze into his. "My ranch?" For years he'd been pestering her to sell her land so he could ruin the gorgeous vistas with a bunch of luxury homes.

To his credit, the look in his hazel eyes remained friendly and compelling despite her antagonism. "Among other things."

"You're wasting your time," she told him yet again. "I'm not selling."

"I never consider the time I spend with you as wasted." Honey dripped from every vowel as he flashed his perfect white teeth in a sexy grin.

Brandee's nerve endings sizzled in response. Several times in the last few years she'd considered hooking up with the cocky charmer. He possessed a body to die for and offered the perfect balance of risk and fun. Sex with him would be explosive and memorable. Too memorable. No doubt she'd spend the rest of her days wanting more. Except as far as she could tell, Shane wasn't the type to stick around for long. Not that she was looking for anything long-term, but a girl could get addicted to things that weren't necessarily good for her.

"In fact," he continued, sex appeal rolling off him in waves, "I enjoy our little chats."

"Our chats end up with me turning you down." She gave him her best smirk. "Are you saying you enjoy that?"

"Honey, you know I never back down from a challenge."

At long last he broke eye contact and let his gaze roam over her mouth and breasts. His open appreciation electrified Brandee, leaving her tongue-tied and breathless.

"Good seeing you both." With a nod at Chelsea, Shane ambled away.

"Damn," Chelsea muttered, her tone reverent.

"What?" The question came out a little sharper than Brandee intended. She noticed her hands were clenched and relaxed her fingers. It did no good. Her blood continued to boil, but whether with lust or outrage Brandee couldn't determine.

"You two have some serious chemistry going on. How did I not know this?"

"It's not chemistry," Brandee corrected. "It's antagonism."

"Po-tay-to. Po-tah-to. It's hot." Either Chelsea missed Brandee's warning scowl or she chose to ignore it as she continued, "How come you've never taken him for a test drive?"

"Are you crazy? Did you miss the part where he's been trying to buy Hope Springs Ranch for the last three years?"

"Maybe it's because it gives him an excuse to stop

by and see you? Remember how he came by the day after the tornado and stayed to help?" Two and a half years earlier an F4 tornado had swept through Royal. The biggest to hit in almost eighty years, it had taken out a chunk of the west side of town including the town hall and a wing of Royal Memorial Hospital before raging on to cause various degrees of damage to several surrounding ranches.

"He wasn't being altruistic. He was sniffing around, checking to see if because of the hit the ranch took whether I was in a position where I had to sell."

"That's not why he spent the next few days cleaning up the storm damage."

Brandee shook her head. Chelsea didn't understand how well Shane hid his true motives for being nice to her. He lived by the motto "You catch more flies with honey than vinegar." The smooth-talking son of a bitch wanted Hope Springs Ranch. If Brandee agreed to sell, she'd never hear from Shane again.

"Where Shane Delgado is concerned, let's agree to disagree," Brandee suggested, not wanting to spoil her lunch with further talk of Shane.

"Okay." Chelsea clasped her hands together on the table and leaned forward. "So, tell me your good news. What's going on?"

"I found out this morning that Hope Springs' first summer session is completely booked."

"Brandee, that's fantastic."

Since purchasing the land that had become Hope Springs Ranch, Brandee had been working to create programs for at-risk teens that helped address destructive behaviors and promote self-esteem. Inspired by her own difficult teen years after losing her dad, Brandee wanted to provide a structured, supportive environment for young adults to learn goal-setting, communication and productive life skills.

"I can't believe how well everything is coming together. And how much work I have to do before the bunkhouses and camp facilities are going to be ready."

"You'll get it all done. You're one of the most driven, organized people I know."

"Thanks for the vote of confidence."

It had taken years of hard work and relentless optimism, but she'd done her dad proud with the success she'd made of Hope Springs Ranch. And now she stood on the threshold of realizing her dream of the camp. Her life was perfect and Brandee couldn't imagine anything better than how she felt at this moment.

Shane strode away from his latest encounter with Brandee feeling like he'd been zapped with a cattle prod. Over the years, he'd engaged in many sizzling exchanges with the spitfire rancher. After each one, he'd conned himself into believing he'd emerged unscathed, while in reality he rarely escaped without several holes poked in his ego.

She was never happy to see him. It didn't seem fair when everything about her brightened his day. Usually he stopped by her ranch and caught her laboring beside her ranch hands, moving cattle, tending to the horses or helping to build the structures for her camp. Clad in worn jeans, faded plaid work shirts and dusty boots, her gray-blue eyes blazing in a face streaked with sweat and dirt, she smelled like horses, hay and hard work. All tomboy. All woman. And he lusted after every lean inch of her.

She, however, was completely immune to him. Given her impenetrable defenses, he should have moved on. There were too many receptive women who appreciated that he was easy and fun, while in Brandee's cool gaze, he glimpsed an ocean of distrust.

But it was the challenge of bringing her around. Of knowing that once he drew her beneath his spell, he would satisfy himself with her complete surrender and emerge triumphant. This didn't mean he was a bad guy. He just wasn't built to be tied down. And from what he'd noticed of Brandee's social life, she wasn't much into long-term relationships, either.

And so he kept going back for more despite knowing each time they tangled she would introduce him to some fresh hell. Today it had been the scent of her perfume. A light floral scent that made him long to gather handfuls of her hair and bury his face in the lustrous gold waves.

"Shane."

His mental meanderings came to a screeching halt. He nodded in acknowledgment toward a trio of women, unsure which one had hailed him. These three were trouble. Cecelia, Simone and Naomi. A blonde, brunette and a redhead. All three women were gorgeous, entitled and dangerous if crossed.

They'd recently been admitted to the Texas Cattleman's Club and were making waves with their demands that the clubhouse needed a feminine face-lift. They wanted to get rid of the old boys' club style and weren't being subtle about manipulating votes in their favor.

Brandee had been one of their most obstinate adversaries, working tirelessly to gather the votes needed to defeat them. She'd infiltrated the ranks of the oldest and most established members in order to preach against every suggestion these three women made. The whole thing was amusing to watch.

Shane responded to Naomi's wave by strolling to their table. "Ladies."

"Join us," Cecelia insisted. She was a striking platinum blonde with an ice queen's sharp eyes. As president of To The Moon, a company specializing in high-end children's furniture, Cecelia was obviously accustomed to being obeyed.

Putting on his best easy grin, Shane shook his head. "Now, you know I'd love nothing more, but I'm sorry to say I'm already running late." He glanced to where his best friend, Gabriel Walsh, sat talking on his cell phone, a half-empty tumbler of scotch on the table before him. "Is there something I can do for you ladies?"

"We noticed you were talking with Brandee Lawless," Simone said, leaning forward in a way that offered a sensational glimpse of her ample cleavage. With lush curves, arresting blue eyes and long black hair, she, too, was a striking blend of beauty and brains. "And we wanted to give you some friendly advice about her."

Had the women picked up on his attraction to Brandee? If so, Shane was losing his touch. He set his hands on the back of the empty fourth chair and leaned in with a conspiratorial wink.

"I'm always happy to listen to advice from beautiful women."

Cecelia nodded as if approving his wisdom. "She's only acting interested in you because she wants you to vote against the clubhouse redesign."

Shane blinked. Brandee was acting interested in him? What had these three women seen that he'd missed?

"Once the vote is done," Simone continued, "she will dismiss you like that." She snapped her fingers and settled her full lips into a determined pout.

"Brandee has been acting as if she's interested in me?" Shane put on a show of surprise and hoped this would entice the women to expound on their theories. "I thought she was just being nice."

The women exchanged glances and silently selected Naomi to speak next. "She's not nice. She's manipulating you. Haven't you noticed the way she flirts with you? She knows how well liked you are and plans to use your popularity to manipulate the vote."

Shane considered this. Was Brandee flirting with him? For a second he let himself bask in the pleasure of that idea. Did she fight the same intoxicating attraction that gripped him every time they met? Then he rejected the notion. No. The way she communicated with him was more like a series of verbal jousts all determined to knock him off his white charger and land him ass-first in the dirt.

"Thank you for the warning, ladies." Unnecessary

as it had been. "I'll make sure I keep my wits about me where Brandee is concerned."

"Anytime," Naomi murmured. Her brown eyes, framed by long, lush lashes, had a sharp look of satisfaction.

"We will always have your back," Cecelia added, and glanced at the other two, garnering agreeing head bobs.

"I'll remember that." With a friendly smile and a nod, Shane left the trio and headed to where Gabe waited.

The former Texas Ranger watched him approach, a smirk kicking up one corner of his lips. "What the hell was that about? Were you feeding them canaries?"

"Canaries?" Shane dropped into his seat and gestured to a nearby waiter. He needed a stiff drink after negotiating the gauntlet of strong-willed women.

"That was a trio of very satisfied pussycats."

Shane resisted the urge to rub at the spot between his shoulder blades that burned from several sets of female eyes boring into him. "I gave them what they wanted."

"Don't you always?"

"It's what I do."

Shane flashed a cocky grin, but he didn't feel any satisfaction.

"So what did they want?" Gabe asked.

"To warn me about Brandee Lawless."

Gabe's gaze flickered past Shane. Whatever he saw made his eyes narrow. "Do you need to be warned?"

"Oh hell no." The waiter set a scotch before him

and Shane swallowed a healthy dose of the fiery liquid before continuing. "You know how she and I are. If we were kids she'd knock me down and sit on me."

"And you'd let her because then she'd be close enough to tickle."

"Tickle?" Shane stared at his best friend in mock outrage. "Do you not know me at all?"

"We're talking about you and Brandee as little kids. It was the least offensive thing I could think of that you'd do to her."

Shane snorted in amusement. "You could have said *spank*."

Gabe closed his eyes as if in pain. "Can we get back to Cecelia, Simone and Naomi?"

"They're just frustrated that Brandee has sided against them and has more influence at the club than they do. They want to rule the world. Or at least our little corner of it."

On the table, Gabe's phone chimed, signaling a text. "Damn," he murmured after reading the screen.

"Bad news?"

"My uncle's tumor isn't operable."

Several weeks ago Gabe's uncle Dusty had been diagnosed with stage-four brain cancer.

"Aw, Gabe, I'm sorry. That really sucks."

Dale "Dusty" Walsh was a dynamic bear of a man. Like Gabe he was a few inches over six feet and built to intimidate. Founder of Royal's most private security firm, The Walsh Group, he'd brought Gabe into the fold after he'd left the Texas Rangers.

"Yeah, my dad's pretty shook up. That was him sending the text."

Gabe's close relationship with his father was something Shane had always envied. His dad had died when Shane was in his early twenties, but even before the heart attack took him, there hadn't been much good about their connection.

"Hopefully, the doctors have a good alternative program to get Dusty through this."

"Let's hope."

The two men shifted gears and talked about the progress on Shane's latest project, a luxury resort development in the vein of George Vanderbilt's iconic French Renaissance château in North Carolina, but brimming with cutting-edge technology. As he was expounding on the challenges of introducing the concept of small plates to a state whose motto was "everything's bigger in Texas," a hand settled on Shane's shoulder. The all-too-familiar zap of awareness told him who stood beside him before she spoke.

"Hello, Gabe. How are things at The Walsh Group?"

"Fine." Gabe's hazel eyes took on a devilish gleam as he noticed Shane's gritted teeth. "And how are you doing at Hope Springs?"

"Busy. We've got ninety-two calves on the ground and another hundred and ninety-seven to go before April." Brandee's hand didn't move from Shane's shoulder as she spoke. "Thanks for helping out with the background checks for the latest group of volunteers."

"Anytime."

Shane drank in the soft lilt in Brandee's voice as he

endured the warm press of her hand. He shouldn't be so aware of her, but the rustle of her tulle skirt and the shapely bare legs below the modest hem had his senses all revved up with nowhere to go.

"See you later, boys." Brandee gave Shane's shoulder a little squeeze before letting go.

"Bye, Brandee," Gabe replied, shifting his gaze to Shane as she headed off.

All too aware of Gabe's smirk, Shane summoned his willpower to not turn around and watch her go, but he couldn't resist a quick peek over his shoulder. He immediately wished he'd fought harder. Brandee floated past the tables like a delicate gray cloud. A cloud with badass boots the color of Texas bluebonnets on her feet. He felt the kick to his gut and almost groaned.

"You know she only did that to piss off those three," Gabe said when Shane had turned back around. "They think she's plotting against them, so she added fuel to the fire."

"I know." He couldn't help but admire her clever machinations even though it had come with a hit to his libido. "She's a woman after my own heart."

Gabe laughed. "Good thing you don't have one to give her."

Shane lifted his drink and saluted his friend. "You've got that right."

Two

Afternoon sunlight lanced through the mini blinds covering the broad west-facing window in Brandee's home office, striping the computer keyboard and her fingers as they flew across the keys. She'd been working on the budget for her summer camp, trying to determine where she could siphon off a few extra dollars to buy three more well-trained, kid-friendly horses.

She'd already invested far more in the buildings and infrastructure than she'd initially intended. And because she needed to get the first of three projected bunkhouses built in time for her summer session, she'd been forced to rely on outside labor to get the job done.

Brandee spun her chair and stared out the window that overlooked the large covered patio, with its outdoor kitchen and fieldstone fireplace. She loved spending time outside, even in the winter, and had created a cozy outdoor living room.

Buying this five-thousand-acre parcel outside Royal four years ago had been Brandee's chance to fulfill her father's dream. She hadn't minded having to build a ranch from the ground up after the tornado had nearly wiped her out. In fact, she'd appreciated the clean slate and relished the idea of putting her stamp on the land. She'd set the L-shaped one-story ranch house half a mile off the highway and a quarter mile from the buildings that housed her ranch hands and the outbuildings central to her cow-calving operation.

The original house, built by the previous owner, had been much bigger than this one and poorly designed. Beaux Cook had been a Hollywood actor with grand ideas of becoming a real cowboy. The man had preferred flash over substance, and never bothered to learn anything about the ranching. Within eighteen months, he'd failed so completely as a rancher that Brandee had bought the property for several million less than it was worth.

Brandee was the third owner of the land since it had been lifted from unclaimed status ten years earlier. Emmitt Shaw had been the one who'd secured the parcel adjacent to his ranch by filing a claim and paying the back taxes for the five thousand acres of abandoned land after a trust put into place a century earlier to pay the taxes had run out of money. Health issues had later compelled him to sell off the land to Beaux to pay his medical bills and keep his original ranch running.

However, in the days following the massive storm,

while Brandee was preoccupied with her own devastated property, Shane Delgado had taken advantage of the old rancher's bad health and losses from the tornado to gobble up his ranch to develop luxury homes. If she'd known how bad Beaux's situation had become, she would've offered to buy his land for a fair price.

Instead, she was stuck sharing her property line with his housing development. Brandee liked the raw, untamed beauty of the Texas countryside, and resented Delgado's determination to civilize the landscape with his luxury homes and fancy resort development. Her father had been an old-school cowboy, fond of endless vistas of Texas landscape populated by cattle, rabbits, birds and the occasional mountain lion. He wouldn't be a fan of Shane Delgado's vision for his daughter's property.

Her smartphone chimed, indicating she'd received a text message. There was a phone number, but no name. She read the text and her heart received a potent shock.

Hope Springs Ranch rightfully belongs to Shane Delgado. –Maverick

Too outraged to consider the wisdom of engaging with the mysterious sender, she picked up the phone and texted back.

Who is this and what are you talking about?

Her computer immediately pinged, indicating she'd received an email. She clicked to open the message. It was from Maverick.

Give up your Texas Cattleman's Club membership and wire fifty thousand dollars to the account below or I'll be forced to share this proof of ownership with Delgado. You have two weeks to comply.

Ignoring the bank routing information, Brandee double-clicked on the attachment. It was a scan of a faded, handwritten document, a letter dated March 21, 1899, written by someone named Jasper Crowley. He offered a five-thousand-acre parcel as a dowry to the man who married his daughter, Amelia. From the description of the land, it was the five thousand acres Hope Springs Ranch occupied.

Brandee's outrage dissipated, but uneasiness remained.

This had to be a joke. Nothing about the documentation pointed to Shane. She was ready to dismiss the whole thing when the name Maverick tickled her awareness. Where had she heard it mentioned before? Cecelia Morgan had spoken the name before one of the contentious meetings at the TCC clubhouse. Was Cecelia behind this? Given the demands, it made sense.

Brandee had been doing her best to thwart every power play Cecelia, Simone and Naomi had attempted. There was no way she was going to let the terrible trio bully their way into leadership positions with the Texas Cattleman's Club. Was this their way of getting her to shut up?

She responded to the email.

This doesn't prove anything.

This isn't an empty threat, was the immediate response. Shaw didn't search for Crowley's descendants. I did.

That seemed to indicate that Maverick had proof that Crowley and Shane were related. Okay, so maybe she shouldn't ignore this. Brandee set her hands on the edge of the desk and shoved backward, muttering curses. The office wasn't big enough for her to escape the vile words glowing on the screen, so she got up and left the room to clear her head.

How dare they? She stalked down the hall to the living area, taking in the perfection of her home along the way.

Everything she had was tied up in Hope Springs Ranch. If she wasn't legally entitled to the land, she'd be ruined. Selling the cattle wouldn't provide enough capital for her to start again. And what would become of her camp?

Sweat broke out on Brandee's forehead. Throwing open her front door, she lifted her face to the cool breeze and stepped onto the porch, which ran the full length of her home. Despite the chilly February weather, she settled in a rocker and drew her knees to her chest. Usually contemplating the vista brought her peace. Not today.

What if that document was real and it could be connected to Shane? She dropped her forehead to her knees and groaned. This was a nightmare. Or maybe it was just a cruel trick. The ranch could not belong to Shane Delgado. Whoever Maverick was, and she suspected it was the unholy trio of Cecelia, Simone and Naomi, there was no way this person could be right.

The land had been abandoned. The taxes had ceased being paid. Didn't that mean the acres reverted back to the government? There had to be a process that went into securing unclaimed land. Something that went beyond simply paying the back taxes. Surely Emmitt had followed every rule and procedure. But what if he hadn't? What was she going to do? She couldn't lose Hope Springs Ranch. And especially not to the likes of Shane Delgado.

It took a long time for Brandee's panic to recede. Half-frozen, she retreated inside and began to plan. First on the agenda was to determine if the document was legitimate. Second, she needed to trace Shane back to Jasper Crowley. Third, she needed to do some research on the process for purchasing land that had returned to the government because of unpaid back taxes.

The blackmailer had given her two weeks. It wasn't a lot of time, but she was motivated. And if she proved Shane was the owner of her land? She could comply with Maverick's demands. Fifty thousand wasn't peanuts, but she had way more than that sitting in her contingency fund. She'd pay three times that to keep Shane Delgado from getting his greedy hands on her land.

And if she absolutely had to, she could resign from the Texas Cattleman's Club. She'd earned her membership the same way club members of old had: by making Hope Springs a successful ranch and proving herself a true cattleman. It would eat at her to let Cecelia, Simone and Naomi bully her into giving up the club she deserved to be a part of, but she could yield the high ground if it meant her programs for at-risk teenagers would be able to continue.

Bile rose as she imagined herself facing the trio's triumphant smirks. How many times in school had she stood against the mean girls and kept her pride intact? They'd ridiculed her bohemian style and tormented anyone brave enough to be friends with her. In turn, she'd manipulated their boyfriends into dumping them and exposed their villainous backstabbing to the whole school.

It wasn't something Brandee was proud of, but to be fair, she'd been dealing with some pretty major ugliness at home and hadn't been in the best frame of mind to take the high road.

When it came to taking care of herself, Brandee had learned how to fight dirty from her father's ranch hands. They'd treated her like a little sister and given her tips on how to get the upper hand in any situation. Brandee had found their advice useful after she'd moved in with her mother and had to cope with whatever flavor of the month she'd shacked up with.

Not all her mother's boyfriends had been creeps, but enough of them had turned their greedy gaze Brandee's way to give her a crash course in manipulation as a method of self-preservation.

And now those skills were going to pay off in spades. Because she intended to do whatever it took to save her ranch, and heaven help anyone who got in her way.

* * *

Standing in what would eventually become the grotto at Pure, the spa in his luxury resort project, The Bellamy, Shane was in an unhappy frame of mind. He surveyed the half-finished stacked stone pillars and the coffered ceiling above the narrow hot tub. In several months, Pure would be the most amazing spa Royal had ever seen, offering a modern take on a traditional Roman bath with a series of soothing, luxurious chambers in which guests could relax and revive.

Right now, the place was a disaster.

"I'm offering people the experience of recharging in an expensive, perfectly designed space," Shane reminded his project manager. "What about this particular stone says expensive or perfect?" He held up a sample of the stacked stone. "This is not what I ordered."

"Let me check on it."

"And then there's that." Shane pointed to the coffered ceiling above the hot tub. "That is not the design I approved."

"Let me check on that, as well."

Shane's phone buzzed, reminding him of his next appointment.

"We'll have to pick this up first thing tomorrow." Even though he was reluctant to stop when he had about fifty more details that needed to be discussed, Shane only had fifteen minutes until he was supposed to be at his mother's home for their weekly dinner, and it was a twenty-minute drive to her house.

Shane wound his way through The Bellamy's construction site, seeing something that needed his attention at every turn. He'd teamed with hotelier Deacon Chase to create the architectural masterpiece, and the scope of the project—and the investment—was enormous.

Sitting on fifty-plus acres of lavish gardens, the resort consisted of two hundred and fifty luxury suites, tricked out with cutting-edge technology. The complex also contained fine farm-to-table dining and other amenities. Every single detail had to be perfect.

He texted his mother before he started his truck, letting her know he was going to be delayed, and her snarky response made him smile. Born Elyse Flynn, Shane's mother had left her hometown of Boston at twenty-two with a degree in geoscience, contracted to do a field study of the area near Royal. There, she'd met Shane's father, Landon, and after a whirlwind six-month romance, married him and settled in at Bullseye, the Delgado family ranch.

After Landon died and Shane took over the ranch, Elyse had moved to a home in Pine Valley, the upscale gated community with a clubhouse, pool and eighteen-hole golf course. Although she seemed content in her six-thousand-square-foot house, when Shane began his housing development near Royal, she'd purchased one of the five-acre lots and begun the process of planning her dream home.

Each week when he visited, she had another architectural design for him to look over. In the last year she'd met with no fewer than a dozen designers. Her wish list grew with each new innovation she saw. There were days when Shane wondered if she'd ever settle on a plan. And part of him dreaded that day because he had a feeling she would then become his worst client ever.

When he entered the house, she was standing in the doorway leading to the library, a glass of red wine in her hand.

"There you are at last," she said, waving him over for a kiss. "Come see how brilliant Thomas is. His latest plan is fantastic."

Thomas Kitt was the architect Elyse was currently leaning toward. She hadn't quite committed to his design, but she'd been speaking of him in glowing terms for the last month.

"He's bumped out the kitchen wall six inches and that gives me the extra room I need so I can go for the thirty-inch built-in wine storage. Now I just need to decide if I want to do the one with the drawers so I can store cheese and other snacks or go with the full storage unit."

She handed Shane the glass of wine she'd readied for him and gestured to the plate of appetizers that sat on samples of granite and quartz piled on the coffee table.

Shane crossed to where she'd pinned the latest drawings to a magnetic whiteboard. "I'd go with the full storage. That'll give you room for an extra sixty bottles."

"You're right." Elyse grinned at her son. "Sounds like a trip to Napa is in my future."

"Why don't you wait until we break ground?" At

the rate his mother was changing her mind, he couldn't imagine the project getting started before fall.

"Your father was always the practical one in our family." Elyse's smile faded at the memory of her deceased husband. "But you've really taken over that role. He'd be very proud of you."

Landon Delgado had never been proud of his son.

You've got nothing going for you but a slick tongue and a cocky attitude, his father had always said.

Elyse didn't seem to notice the dip in her son's mood as she continued, "Is it crazy that I like the industrial feel to this unit?" She indicated the brochure on high-end appliances.

Shane appreciated how much fun his mother was having with the project. He wrapped his arm around her and dropped a kiss on her head. "Whatever you decide is going to be a showstopper."

"I hope so. Suzanne has been going on and on about the new house she's building in your development to the point where I want to throw her and that pretentious designer she hired right through a plate-glass window."

Growing up with four older brothers gave Elyse a competitive spirit in constant need of a creative outlet. Her husband hadn't shared her interests. Landon Delgado had liked ranching and believed in hard work over fancy innovation. He'd often spent long hours in the saddle moving cattle or checking fences. His days began before sunup and rarely ended until long after dinner. When he wasn't out and about on the ranch, he could be found in his office tending to the business side.

To Landon's dismay, Shane hadn't inherited his father's love of all things ranching. Maybe that was because as soon as Shane could sit up by himself, his father had put him on a horse, expecting Shane to embrace the ranching life. But he'd come to hate the way his every spare moment was taken up by ranch duties assigned to him by his father.

You aren't going to amount to anything if you can't handle a little hard work.

About the time he'd hit puberty, Shane's behavior around the ranch had bloomed into full-on rebellion, and when Shane turned fifteen, the real battles began. He started hanging out with older friends who had their own cars. Most days he didn't come home right after school and dodged all his chores. His buddies liked to party. He'd been forced to toil alongside his father since he was three years old. Didn't he deserve to have a little fun?

According to his father, the answer was no.

You're wrong if you think that grin of yours is all you need to make it in this world.

"So what have you cooked up for us tonight?" Shane asked as he escorted his mother to the enormous kitchen at the back of the house.

"Apricot-and-Dijon-glazed salmon." Although Elyse employed a full-time housekeeper, she enjoyed spending time whipping up gourmet masterpieces. "I got the recipe from the man who catered Janice Hunt's dinner party. I think I'm going to hire him to cater the Bullseye's centennial party," Elyse continued, arching an eyebrow at her son's blank expression.

Shane's thoughts were so consumed with The Bellamy project these days, he'd forgotten all about the event. "The centennial party. When is that again?"

"March twenty-first. I've arranged a tasting with Vincent on the twenty-fourth of this month so we can decide what we're going to have."

"We?" He barely restrained a groan. "Don't you have one of your friends who could help with this?"

"I do, but this is *your* ranch we're celebrating and *your* legacy."

"Sure. Of course." Shane had no interest in throwing a big party for the ranch, but gave his mother his best smile. "A hundred years is a huge milestone and we will celebrate big."

This seemed to satisfy his mother. Elyse was very social. She loved to plan parties and when Shane was growing up there had often been dinners with friends and barbecues out by the pool. Often Shane had wondered how a vibrant, beautiful urbanite like his mother had found happiness with an overly serious, rough-around-the-edges Texas rancher. But there was no question that in spite of their differences, his parents had adored each other, and the way Landon had doted on his wife was the one area where Shane had seen eye to eye with his father.

At that moment Brandee Lawless popped into his mind. There was a woman he wanted to sweep into his arms and never let go. He imagined sending her hat spinning away and tunneling his fingers through her long golden hair as he pulled her toward him for a hot, sexy kiss.

But he'd noticed her regarding him with the same skepticism he used to glimpse in his father's eyes. She always seemed to be peering beyond his charm and wit to see what he was made of. He'd never been able to fool her with the mask he showed to the world. It was unsettling. When she looked at him, she seemed to expect…more.

Someday people are going to figure out that you're all show and no substance.

So far he'd been lucky and that hadn't happened. But where Brandee was concerned, it sure seemed like his luck was running out.

Three

After snatching too few hours of sleep, Brandee rushed through her morning chores and headed to Royal's history museum. She hadn't taken time for breakfast and now the coffee she'd consumed on the drive into town was eating away at her stomach lining. Bile rose in her throat as she parked in the museum lot and contemplated her upside-down world.

It seemed impossible that her life could implode so easily. That the discovery of a single piece of paper meant she could lose everything. In the wee hours of the morning as she stared at the ceiling, she'd almost convinced herself to pay Maverick the money and resign from the TCC. Saving her ranch was more important than besting the terrible trio. But she'd never been a quitter and backing down when bullied had never been her style. Besides, as authentic as the document had looked, there was no reason to believe it was real or that it was in the museum where anyone could stumble on it.

Thirty minutes later, she sat at a table in the small reference room and had her worst fears realized. Before her, encased in clear plastic, was the document she'd been sent a photo of. She tore her gaze from the damning slip of paper and looked up at the very helpful curator. From Rueben Walker's surprise when she'd been waiting on the doorstep for the museum to open, Brandee gathered he wasn't used to having company first thing in the morning.

"You say this is part of a collection donated to the museum after Jasper Crowley's death?" Brandee wondered what other bombshells were to be found in the archives.

"Yes, Jasper Crowley was one of the founding members of the Texas Cattleman's Club. Unfortunately he didn't live to see the grand opening of the clubhouse in 1910."

"What other sorts of things are in the collection?"

"The usual. His marriage license to Sarah McKellan. The birth certificate for their daughter, Amelia. Sarah's death certificate. She predeceased Jasper by almost thirty years and he never remarried. Let's see, there were bills of sale for various things. Letters between Sarah and her sister, Lucy, who lived in Austin."

Brandee was most interested in Jasper's daughter. The land had been her dowry. Why hadn't she claimed it?

"Is there anything about what happened to Amelia? Did she ever get married?"

Walker regarded Brandee, his rheumy blue eyes going suddenly keen. "I don't recall there being anything about a wedding. You could go through the newspaper archives. With someone of Jasper's importance, his daughter's wedding would have been prominently featured."

Brandee had neither the time nor the patience for a random search through what could potentially be years' worth of newspapers. "I don't suppose you know of anyone who would be interested in helping me with the research? I'd be happy to compensate them."

"I have a part-time assistant that comes in a few times a week. He might be able to assist you as soon as he gets back from helping his sister move to Utah."

"When will that be?"

"Middle of next week, I think."

Unfortunately, Maverick had only given her two weeks to meet the demands, and if the claims were true, she needed to find out as soon as possible. Brandee ground her teeth and weighed her options.

"Are the newspaper archives here?"

The curator shook his head. "They're over at the library on microfiche."

"Thanks for your help." Brandee gave Reuben a quick nod before exiting the building and crossing the street.

The library was a couple blocks down and it didn't make sense for her to move her truck. She neared Royal Diner and her stomach growled, reminding her she hadn't eaten breakfast. As impatient as she was to get to the bottom of Maverick's claim, she would function better without hunger pangs.

Stepping into Royal Diner was like journeying back in time to the 1950s. Booths lined one wall, their red faux leather standing out against the black-and-white-checkerboard tile floor. On the opposite side of the long aisle stretched the counter with seats that matched the booths.

Not unexpectedly, the place was packed. Brandee spotted local rancher and town pariah, Adam Haskell, leaving the counter toward the back and headed that way, intending to grab his seat. As she drew closer, Brandee noticed a faint scent of stale alcohol surrounded Haskell. She offered him the briefest of nods, which he didn't see because his blue bug-eyes dropped to her chest as they passed each other in the narrow space.

Once clear of Haskell, Brandee saw that the spot she'd been aiming for was sandwiched between an unfamiliar fortysomething cowboy and Shane Delgado. Of all the bad luck. Brandee almost turned tail and ran, but knew she'd look silly doing so after coming all this way. Bracing herself, she slid onto the seat.

Shane glanced up from his smartphone and grinned as he spotted her. "Well, hello. Look who showed up to make my morning."

His deep voice made her nerve endings shiver, and when she bumped her shoulder against his while sliding her purse onto the conveniently placed hook beneath the counter, the hairs on her arms stood up. Hating how her body reacted to him, Brandee shot Shane a sharp glance.

"I'm not in the mood to argue with you." She spoke with a little more bluntness than usual and his eyes widened slightly. "Can we just have a casual conversation about the weather or the price of oil?"

"I heard it's going to be in the midfifties all week," he said, with one of his knockout grins that indicated he liked that he got under her skin. "With a thirty percent chance of rain."

"We could use some rain."

Heidi dropped off Shane's breakfast and took Brandee's order of scrambled eggs, country potatoes and bacon. A second later the waitress popped back with a cup of coffee.

"Everything tasting okay?" Heidi asked Shane, her eyes bright and flirty.

"Perfect as always."

"That's what I like to hear."

When she walked off, Brandee commented, "You haven't taken a single bite. How do you know it's perfect?"

"Because I eat breakfast here twice a week and it's always the same great food." Shane slid his fork into his sunny-side up eggs and the bright yellow yolk ran all over the hash on his plate.

Brandee sipped her coffee and shuddered.

"What's the matter?" Shane's even white teeth bit into a piece of toast. He hadn't looked at her, yet he seemed to know she was bothered.

"Nothing." Brandee tried to keep her voice neutral. "Why?"

"You are looking more disgusted with me than usual." His crooked smile made her pulse hiccup.

"It's the eggs. I can't stand them runny like that." The same flaw in human nature that made people gawk at car accidents was drawing Brandee's gaze back to Shane's plate. She shuddered again.

"Really?" He pushed the yolk around as if to torment her with the sight. "But this is the only way to eat them with corn-beef hash."

"Why corn-beef hash and not biscuits and gravy?"

"It's a nod to my Irish roots."

"You're Irish?"

"On my mother's side. She's from Boston."

"Oh." She drew out her reply as understanding dawned.

"Oh, what?"

"I always wondered about your accent."

"You thought about me?" He looked delighted.

Brandee hid her irritation. Give the man any toehold and he would storm her battlements in a single bound.

"I thought about your accent," she corrected him. "It has a trace of East Coast in it."

Shane nodded. "It's my mom's fault. Even after living in Texas for nearly forty years, she still drops her *r*'s most of the time."

"How'd your mom come to live in Texas?"

Even as Brandee asked the question, it occurred to her that this was the most normal conversation she and Shane had ever had. Usually they engaged in some sort of verbal sparring or just outright arguing and rarely traded any useful information.

"She came here after college to study oil reserves and met my dad. They were married within six months and she's been here ever since." Shane used his toast to clean up the last of the egg. "She went back to Boston after my dad died and stayed for almost a year, but found she missed Royal."

"I'm sure it was you that she missed."

Shane nodded. "I am the apple of her eye."

"Of course." Brandee thanked Heidi as the waitress set a plate down on the counter. With the arrival of her breakfast, Brandee had intended to let her side of the conversation lapse, but something prompted her to ask, "She didn't remarry?"

Never in a million years would Brandee admit it, but Shane's story about his mother was interesting. Shane's father had died over a decade earlier, but Elyse Delgado had accompanied her son to several events at the TCC clubhouse since Brandee had bought Hope Springs Ranch. Her contentious relationship with Shane caused Brandee to avoid him in social situations and she'd never actually spoken to his mother except to say hello in passing. Yet, Brandee knew Elyse Delgado by reputation and thought she would've enjoyed getting to know the woman better if not for her son.

"There've been a couple men she's dated, but nothing serious has come out of it. Although she was completely devoted to my father, I think she's enjoyed her independence."

"I get that," Brandee murmured. "I like the freedom to run my ranch the way I want and not having to worry about taking anyone's opinions into account."

"You make it sound as if you never plan to get married." Shane sounded surprised and looked a little dismayed. "That would certainly be a shame."

Brandee's hackles rose. He probably hadn't intended to strike a nerve, but in the male-dominated world of Texas cattle ranching, she'd faced down a lot of chauvinism.

"I don't need a man to help me or complete me."

At her hot tone, Shane threw up his hands. "That's not what I meant."

"No?" She snorted. "Tell me you don't look at me and wonder how I handle Hope Springs Ranch without a man around." She saw confirmation in his body language before he opened his mouth to argue. "Thanks to my dad, I know more about what it takes to run a successful ranch than half the men around here."

"I don't doubt that."

"But you still think I need someone."

"Yes." Shane's lips curved in a sexy grin. "If only to kiss you senseless and take the edge off that temper of yours."

The second Brandee's eyes cooled, Shane knew he should've kept his opinion to himself. They'd been having a perfectly nice conversation and he'd had to go and ruin it. But all her talk of not needing a man around had gotten under his skin. He wasn't sure why.

"I have neither a temper nor an edge." Brandee's

conversational tone wasn't fooling Shane. "Ask anyone in town and they'll tell you I'm determined, but polite."

"Except when I'm around."

Her expression relaxed. "You do bring out the worst in me."

And for some reason she brought out the worst in him. "I'd like to change that." But first he had to learn to hold his tongue around her.

"Why?"

"Because you interest me."

"As someone who sees through your glib ways?"

"I'll admit you've presented a challenge." Too many things in his life came easily. He didn't have to exert himself chasing the unachievable. But in Brandee's case, he thought the prize might be worth the extra effort.

"I've begun to wonder if convincing me to sell Hope Springs had become a game to you."

"I can't deny that I'd like your land to expand my development, but that's not the only reason I'm interested in you."

"Is it because I won't sleep with you?"

He pretended to be surprised. "That never even occurred to me. I'm still in the early stages of wooing you."

"Wooing?" Her lips twitched as if she were fighting a smile. "You do have a way with words, Shane Delgado."

"Several times you've accused me of having a silver tongue. I might have a knack for smooth talking, but that doesn't mean I'm insincere."

Brandee pushed her unfinished breakfast away and gave him her full attention. "Let me get this straight. You want us to date?" She laughed before he could answer.

He'd thought about it many times, but never with serious intent. Their chemistry was a little too combustible, more like a flash bang than a slow burn, and he'd reached a point in his life where he liked to take his time with a woman.

"Whoa," he said, combating her skepticism with lighthearted banter. "Let's not get crazy. How about we try a one-week cease-fire and see how things go?"

Her features relaxed into a genuine smile and Shane realized she was relieved. His ego took a hit. Had she been dismayed that he'd viewed her in a romantic light? Most women would be thrilled. Once again he reminded himself that she was unique and he couldn't approach her the same way he did every other female on the planet.

"Does that mean you're not going to try to buy Hope Springs for a week?" Despite her smile, her eyes were somber as she waited for his answer.

"Sure."

"Let's make it two weeks, then."

To his surprise, she held out her hand like it was some sort of legal agreement. Shane realized that for all their interaction, they'd never actually touched skin to skin. The contact didn't disappoint.

Pleasure zipped up his arm and lanced straight through his chest. If he hadn't been braced against the shock, he might have let slip a grunt of surprise.

Her grip was strong. Her slender fingers bit into his hand without much effort on her part. He felt the work-roughened calluses on her palm and the silky-smooth skin on the back of her hand. It was a study in contrasts, like everything else about her.

Desire ignited even as she let go and snatched up her bill. With an agile shift of her slim body, she was sliding into the narrow space between his chair and hers. Her chest brushed his upper arm and he felt the curve of her breasts even through the layers of her sweater and his jacket.

"See you, Delgado."

Before he got his tongue working again, she'd scooped her coat and purse off the back of the chair and was headed for the front cash register. Helpless with fascination, he watched her go, enjoying the unconscious sashay of her firm, round butt encased in worn denim. The woman knew how to make an exit.

"Damn," he murmured, signaling to the waitress that he wanted his coffee topped off. He had a meeting in half an hour, but needed to calm down before he headed out.

A cup of coffee later, he'd recovered enough to leave. As he looked for his bill, he realized it was missing. He'd distinctly recalled Heidi sliding it onto the counter, but now it was gone. He caught her eye and she came over with the coffeepot.

"More coffee, Shane?"

"No, I've got to get going, but I don't see my bill and wondered if it ended up on the floor over there." He indicated her side of the counter.

"All taken care of."

"I don't understand."

"Brandee got it."

Had that been the reason for her brush by? In the moment, he'd been so preoccupied by her proximity that he hadn't been aware of anything else. And he understood why she'd paid for his meal. She was announcing that she was independent and his equal. It also gave her a one-up on him.

"Thanks, Heidi." In a pointless assertion of his masculinity, he slid a ten-dollar tip under the sugar dispenser before heading out the door.

As he headed to his SUV, he considered his action. Would he have been compelled to leave a large tip if Gabe or Deacon had picked up his tab? Probably not. Obviously it bothered him to have a woman pay for his meal. Or maybe it wasn't just any woman, but a particular woman who slipped beneath his skin at every turn.

Why had he rejected the idea of dating her so fast? In all likelihood they'd drive each other crazy in bed. And when it was over, things between them would be no worse. Seemed he had nothing to lose and a couple months of great sex to gain.

As he headed to The Bellamy site to see how the project was going, Shane pondered how best to approach Brandee. She wasn't the sort to be wowed with the things he normally tried and she'd already declared herself disinterested in romantic entanglements. Or had she?

Shane found himself back at square one, and realized just how difficult the task before him was. Yet he didn't shy from the challenge. In fact, the more he thought about dating Brandee, the more determined he became to convince her to give them a shot.

But how did a man declare his intentions when the woman was skeptical of every overture?

The answer appeared like the sun breaking through the clouds. It involved the project nearest and dearest to her heart: Hope Springs Camp for at-risk and troubled teenagers. He would somehow figure out what she needed most and make sure she got it. By the time he was done, she would be eating out of his hands.

Brandee left the Royal Diner after paying for Shane's breakfast, amusing herself by pondering how much it would annoy him when he found out what she'd done. She nodded a greeting to several people as she headed to the library. Once there, however, all her good humor fled as she focused on finding out whether there was any truth to Maverick's assertion that Shane was a direct descendant of Amelia Crowley.

It took her almost five hours and she came close to giving up three separate times, but at long last she traced his family back to Jasper Crowley. Starting with newspapers from the day Jasper had penned the dowry document, she'd scrolled through a mile of microfiche until she'd found a brief mention of Amelia, stating that she'd run off with a man named Tobias Stone.

Using the Stone family name, Brandee then tracked down a birth certificate for their daughter Beverly. The Stones hadn't settled near Royal but had ended up two counties over. But the state of Texas had a good database of births and deaths, and the town where they'd ended up had all their newspapers' back issues online.

Jumping forward seventeen years, she began reading newspapers again for some notice of Beverly Stone's marriage. She'd been debating giving up on the newspapers and driving to the courthouse when her gaze fell on the marriage announcement. Beverly had married Charles Delgado and after that Brandee's search became a whole lot easier.

At last she was done. Spread across the table, in unforgiving black and white, was the undeniable proof that Shane Delgado was legally entitled to the land where Hope Springs Ranch stood. A lesser woman would have thrown herself a fine pity party. Brandee sat dry-eyed and stared at Shane's birth certificate. It was the last piece of the puzzle.

In a far more solemn mood than when she'd arrived, Brandee exited the library. The setting sun cast a golden glow over the street. Her research had eaten up the entire day, and she felt more exhausted than if she'd rounded up and tagged a hundred cattle all on her own. She needed a hot bath to ease the tension in her shoulders and a large glass of wine to numb her emotions.

But most of all she wanted to stop thinking about Shane Delgado and his claim to her land for a short time. Unfortunately, once she'd settled into her bath, and as the wine started a warm buzz through her veins, that proved impossible. Dwelling on the man while lying naked in a tub full of bubbles was counterproductive. So was mulling over their breakfast conversation at the Royal Diner, but she couldn't seem to shake the look in his eye as he'd talked about kissing her senseless.

She snorted. As if her current problems could be forgotten beneath the man's chiseled lips and strong hands. She closed her eyes and relived the handshake. The contact had left her palm tingling for nearly a minute. As delightful as the sensation had been, what had disturbed her was how much she'd liked touching him. How she wouldn't mind letting her hands wander all over his broad shoulders and tight abs.

With a groan Brandee opened her eyes and shook off her sensual daydreams. Even if Shane wasn't at the center of her biggest nightmare, she couldn't imagine either one of them letting go and connecting in any meaningful way.

But maybe she didn't need meaningful. Maybe what she needed was to get swept up in desire and revel in being female. She'd deny it until she was hoarse, but it might be nice to let someone be in charge for a little while. And if that someone was Shane Delgado? At least she'd be in for an exhilarating ride.

The bathwater had cooled considerably while Brandee's mind had wandered all over Shane's impressive body. She came out of her musings to discover she'd lost an hour and emerged from her soaking tub with pruney fingers and toes.

While she was toweling off, her office phone began to ring. It was unusual to have anyone calling the ranch in the evening, but not unheard-of. After she'd dressed in an eyelet-trimmed camisole and shorts sleepwear set she'd designed, Brandee padded down the hall to her office, curled up in her desk chair and dialed into voice mail.

"I heard you're looking for a couple horses for your summer camp." The voice coming from the phone's speaker belonged to Shane Delgado. "I found one that might work for you. Liam Wade has a champion reining horse that he had to retire from showing because of his bad hocks. He wants the horse to go to a good home and is interested in donating him to your cause."

Brandee had a tight budget to complete all her projects and was doing a pretty good job sticking to it. When she'd first decided to start a camp, she'd done a few mini-events to see how things went. That was how she'd funded the meeting hall where she served meals and held classes during the day and where the kids could socialize in the evenings. Thanks to her successes, she'd forged ahead with her summer-camp idea. But that required building a bunkhouse that could sleep twelve.

With several minor issues leading to overages she'd hadn't planned for, getting a high-quality, well-trained horse for free from Liam Wade would be awesome. She already had three other horses slated for the camp and hoped to have six altogether to start.

Brandee picked up the phone and dialed Shane back. Knees drawn up to her chest, she waited for him to answer and wondered what he'd expect in return for this favor.

After three rings Shane picked up. "I take it you're interested in the horse."

"Very." Her toes curled over the edge of the leather cushion of her desk chair as his deep, rich voice filled her ear. "Thank you for putting this together."

"My pleasure."

"It was really nice of you." Remembering that he had the power to destroy all she'd built didn't stop her from feeling grateful. "I guess I owe you…" She grasped at the least problematic way she could pay him back.

"You don't owe me a thing."

Immediately Brandee went on alert. He hadn't demanded dinner or sexual favors in exchange for his help. What was this new game he was playing? Her thoughts turned to the blackmailer Maverick. Once again she wondered whether Shane was involved, but quickly rejected the idea. If he had any clue she was squatting on land that belonged to his family, he would be up front about his intentions.

"Well, then," she muttered awkwardly. "Thank you."

"Happy to help."

After hanging up, she spent a good ten minutes staring at the phone. Happy to help? That rang as false as his "you don't owe me a thing." What was he up to? With no answers appearing on the horizon, Brandee returned to her bedroom and settled in to watch some TV, but nothing held her attention.

She headed into the kitchen for a cup of Sleepytime herbal tea, but after consuming it, she was more wide-awake than ever. So she started a load of laundry and killed another hour with some light housekeeping. As the sole occupant of the ranch house, Brandee only had her cook and cleaning woman, May, come in a couple times a week.

Standing in the middle of her living room, Brandee surveyed her home with a sense of near despair and cursed Maverick. If she found out who was behind the blackmail, she'd make sure they paid. In the meantime, she had to decide what to do. She sank down onto her couch and pulled a cotton throw around her shoulders.

Her choice was clear. She had to pay the fifty thousand dollars and resign from the Texas Cattleman's Club. As much as it galled her to give in, she couldn't risk losing her home. She pictured the smug satisfaction on the faces of the terrible trio and ground her teeth together.

And if Maverick wasn't one or all of them?

What if she'd read the situation wrong and someone else was behind the extortion? She had no guarantee that if she met the demands that Maverick wouldn't return to the well over and over. The idea of spending the rest of her life looking over her shoulder or paying one blackmail demand after another appalled Brandee. But what could she do?

Her thoughts turned to Shane once more. What if she could get him to give up his claim to the land? She considered what her father would think of the idea and shied away from the guilt that aroused. Buck Lawless had never cheated or scammed anyone and would be ashamed of his daughter for even considering it.

But then, Buck had never had to endure the sort of environment Brandee had been thrust into after his death. In her mother's house, Brandee had received a quick and unpleasant education in self-preservation. Her father's position as ranch foreman had meant that Brandee could live and work among the ranch hands and never worry that they'd harm her. That hadn't been the case with her mother's various boyfriends.

She wasn't proud that she'd learned how to manipulate others' emotions and desires, but she was happy to have survived that dark time and become the successful rancher her father had always hoped she'd be. As for what she was going to do about Shane? What he didn't know about his claim on Hope Springs Ranch wouldn't hurt him. She just needed to make sure he stayed in the dark until she could figure out a way to keep her land free and clear.

Four

At Bullseye Ranch's main house, Shane sat on the leather sofa in the den, boots propped on the reclaimed wood coffee table, an untouched tumbler of scotch dangling from the fingers of his left hand. Almost twenty-four hours had gone by since Brandee had called to thank him for finding her a horse and he'd been thinking about her almost nonstop. She'd sounded wary on the phone, as if expecting him to demand something in return for his help. It wasn't the response he'd been hoping for, but it was pure Brandee.

What the hell was wrong with the woman that she couldn't accept a kind gesture? Well, to be fair, he hadn't acted with pure altruism. He did want something from her, but it wasn't what she feared. His motive was personal not business. Would she ever believe that?

His doorbell rang. Shane set aside his drink and went to answer the door. He wasn't expecting visitors.

It was Brandee standing on his front porch. The petite blonde was wearing her customary denim and carrying a bottle wrapped in festive tissue. She smiled at his shocked look, obviously pleased to have seized the upper hand for the moment.

"Brought you a little thank-you gift," she explained, extending the bottle. "I know you like scotch and thought you might appreciate this."

"Thanks." He gestured her inside and was more than a little bewildered when she strolled past him.

"Nice place you have here." Brandee shoved her hands into the back pockets of her jeans as she made her way into the middle of the living room.

"I can't take the credit. My mom did all the remodeling and design."

"She should have been an interior designer."

"I've told her that several times." Shane peeled the paper off the bottle and whistled when he saw the label. "This is a great bottle of scotch."

"Glad you like it. I asked the bartender at the TCC clubhouse what he'd recommend and this is what he suggested."

"Great choice." The brand was far more expensive than anything Shane had in his house and he was dying to try it. "Will you join me in a drink?"

"Just a short one. I have to drive home."

Shane crossed to the cabinet where he kept his liquor and barware. He poured shots into two tulip-shaped glasses with short, stout bases and handed her one.

Brandee considered it with interest. "I thought you drank scotch from tumblers."

"Usually, but you brought me a special scotch," he said, lifting his glass to the light and assessing the color. "And it deserves a whiskey glass."

"What should we drink to?" she asked, snagging his gaze with hers.

Mesmerized by the shifting light in her blue-gray eyes, he said the first bit of nonsense that popped into his head. "World peace?"

"To world peace." With a nod she tapped her glass lightly against his.

Before Shane drank, he gave the scotch a good swirl to awaken the flavors. He then lifted the glass to his nose and sniffed. A quality scotch like this was worth taking the time to appreciate. He took a healthy sip and rolled it around his tongue. At last he swallowed it, breathed deeply and waited. At around the six-second mark, the richness of the scotch rose up and blessed him with all its amazing flavors—citrus, pears, apples and plums from the sherry barrels it was aged in, along with an undertone of chocolate and a hint of licorice at the very end.

"Fantastic," he breathed.

Brandee watched him with open curiosity, then held up her glass. "I've never been much of a scotch drinker, but watching you just now makes me think I've been missing out. Teach me to enjoy it."

She couldn't have said anything that pleased him more.

"I'd be happy to. First of all you want to swirl the

scotch in the glass and then sniff it. Unlike wine, what you smell is what you'll taste."

She did as he instructed, taking her time about it. "Now what?"

"Now you're going to take a big mouthful." He paused while she did as instructed. "That's it. Get it onto the middle of your tongue. You'll begin to tease out the spice and the richness." He let her experience the scotch for a few more seconds and then said, "Take a big breath, swallow and open your mouth. Now wait for it."

She hadn't blinked, which was good. If she had, it would mean the scotch flavor was too strong. Her expression grew thoughtful and then her eyes flared with understanding.

"I get it. Tangerine and plum."

"The second sip is even better."

Together they took their second taste. The pleasure Shane received was doubled because he was able to share the experience with Brandee. She didn't roll her eyes or make faces like many women of his acquaintance would have. Instead, she let him lead her through an exploration of all the wonderful subtleties of the scotch.

Fifteen minutes later, they had reached a level of connection unprecedented in their prior four years of knowing each other. He was seeing a new side of Brandee. A delightful, sociable side that had him patting himself on the back for putting her in touch with Liam. Convincing her they should give dating a try was going to be way easier than he'd originally thought.

Brandee finished her last sip of scotch and set the glass aside. "I had another reason for dropping by tonight other than to say thank-you."

Shane waited in silence for her to continue, wondering if the other shoe was about to drop.

"I thought about what you said in the diner yesterday." She spoke slowly as if she'd put a lot of thought into what she was saying.

Shane decided to help her along. "About you needing to be kissed senseless?" He grinned when he saw the gap between her eyebrows narrow.

"About us calling a truce for two weeks," she countered, her tone repressive. "I know how you are and I realized that after those two weeks, you'd be back to pestering me to sell the ranch."

Right now, he didn't really give a damn about buying her ranch, but he sensed if he stopped pestering her about it she would forget all about him. "You have a solution for that?"

"I do. I was thinking about a wager."

Now she was speaking his language. "What sort of wager?"

"If I win you agree to give up all current and future attempts to claim Hope Springs Ranch and its land."

"And if I win?"

"I'll sell you my ranch."

A silence settled between them so loud Shane could no longer hear the television in the den. Unless she was convinced she had this wager all sewn up, this was a preposterous offer for her to make. What was she up to?

"Let me get this straight," he began, wanting to

make sure he'd heard her clearly. "After years of re-fusing to sell me your land, you're suddenly ready to put it on the table and risk losing it?" He shook his head. "I don't believe it. You love that ranch too much to part with it so easily."

"First of all, what makes you think you're going to win? You haven't even heard the terms."

He arched one eyebrow. "And the second thing?"

"I said I'd sell the land. I didn't say how much I wanted for it."

He'd known all along that she was clever and rel-ished the challenge of pitting his wits against hers. "Ten million. That's more than fair market value."

Her blue-gray eyes narrowed. She'd never get that much from anyone else and they both knew it.

"Fine. Ten million."

The speed with which she agreed made Shane won-der what he'd gotten himself into. "And the terms of our wager?"

"Simple." A sly smile bloomed. "For two weeks you move in and help me out at the ranch. Between calv-ing time and the construction project going on at my camp, I'm stretched thin."

Shane almost laughed in relief. This was not at all what he'd thought she'd propose. Did she think he'd shy away from a couple weeks of manual labor? Granted, he rarely came home with dirt beneath his fingernails, but that didn't mean he was lazy or incompetent. He knew which end of the hammer to use.

"You need someone who knows his way around a

power tool." He shot her a lecherous grin. "I'm your man."

"And I need you to help with the minicamp I have going next weekend."

Now he grasped her logic. She intended to appeal to his altruistic side. She probably figured if he got a close look at her troubled-teen program that he would give up trying to buy the land. This was a bet she was going to lose. He didn't give a damn about a camp for a bunch of screwed-up kids who probably didn't need anything more than parents who knew how to set boundaries.

"That's it?" He was missing something, but he wasn't sure what. "I move in and help you out?" Living with Brandee was like a dream come true. He could survive a few backbreaking days of hard work if it meant plenty of time to convince her they could be good together for a while.

"I can see where your mind has gone and yes…" She paused for effect. "You'll have ample opportunity to convince me to sleep with you."

A shock as potent as if he'd grabbed a live wire with both hands blasted through him. His nerve endings tingled in the aftermath. He struggled to keep his breathing even as he considered the enormity of what she'd just offered.

"You call that a wager?" He had no idea where he found the strength to joke. "I call it shooting ducks in a barrel."

"Don't you mean fish?" Her dry smile warned him winning wasn't going to be easy. "Getting me to sleep with you isn't the wager. You were right when you said I was lacking male companionship."

Well, smack my ass and call me a newborn. The phrase, often repeated by Shane's grandma Bee, popped into his head unbidden. He coughed to clear his throat.

"I said you needed to be kissed senseless."

She rolled her eyes at him. "Yes. Yes. It's been a while since I dated anyone. And I'll admit the thought of you and I has crossed my mind once or twice."

"Damn, woman. You sure do know how to stroke a man's ego."

"Oh please," she said. "You love playing games. I thought this would appeal to everything you stand for."

"And what is that exactly?"

"You get me to say I love you and I sell you the ranch for ten million."

He hadn't prepared himself properly for the devastation of that other shoe. It was a doozy. "And what needs to happen for you to win?"

"Simple." Her smile was pure evil. "I get you to say 'I love you' to me."

Brandee stood on her front porch, heart beating double-time, and watched Shane pull a duffel out of his SUV. In his other hand he held a laptop case. It was late afternoon the day after Brandee had pitched her ridiculous wager to Shane and he was moving in.

This was without a doubt the stupidest idea she'd ever had. Paying Maverick the blackmail money and quitting the TCC was looking better and better. But how would she explain her abrupt change of heart to

Shane? No doubt he would consider her backpedaling proof that she was afraid of losing her heart to him.

At least she didn't have to worry about that happening. There was only room in her life for her ranch and her camp. Maybe in a couple years when things settled down she could start socializing. She'd discovered that as soon as she'd started thinking about seducing Shane, a floodgate to something uncomfortably close to loneliness had opened wide.

"Hey, roomie," he called, taking her porch steps in one easy bound.

Involuntarily she stepped back as he came within a foot of her. His wolfish grin was an acknowledgment of her flinch.

"Welcome to Hope Springs Ranch."

"Glad to be here."

"Let me show you to your room. Dinner's at seven. Breakfast is at six. I don't know what you're used to, but we get up early around here."

"Early to bed. Early to rise. I can get on board with the first part. The second may take some getting used to."

Brandee let out a quiet sigh. Shane's not-so-subtle sexual innuendo was going to get old really fast. It might be worth sleeping with him right away to get that to stop.

"I'm sure you'll manage." She led the way into the ranch house and played tour guide. "Kitchen. Dining room. Living room."

"Nice." Shane took his time gazing around the un-cluttered open-plan space.

"Your room is this way." She led him into a hallway and indicated a door on the left. "Guest bedrooms one and two share that bathroom. I put you in the guest suite. It has its own bathroom and opens to the patio."

Shane entered the room she indicated and set his duffel on the king-size bed. "Nice."

The suite was decorated in the same neutral tones found throughout the rest of the house. It was smaller than her master bedroom, but she'd lavished the same high-end materials on it.

"You'll be comfortable, then?" She imagined his master suite at Bullseye was pretty spectacular given what she'd seen of his living room.

"Very comfortable." He circled the bed and stared out the French doors. "So where do you sleep?"

He asked the question with no particular inflection, but her body reacted as if he'd swept her into his arms. She shoved her hands into her back pockets to conceal their trembling and put on her game face. She'd get nowhere with him if he noticed how easily he could provoke her.

"I'll show you."

Cringing at the thought of inviting him into her personal space, Brandee nevertheless led the way back down the hall and past the kitchen. When she'd worked with the architect, she insisted the master suite be isolated from the guest rooms. Passing her home office, Brandee gestured at it as she went by and then strode into her private sanctuary. It wasn't until Shane stood in the middle of her space, keen eyes taking in every detail, that she realized the magnitude of her mistake.

It wasn't that giving him a glimpse of her bedroom might clue him in to what made her tick. Or even that she'd imagined him making love to her here. It was far worse than that. She discovered that she liked having him in her space. She wanted to urge him into one of the chairs that faced her cozy fireplace and stretch out in its twin with her bare feet on his lap, letting him massage the aches from her soles with his strong fingers.

"Nice."

Apparently this was his go-to word for all things related to decorating. She chuckled, amusement helping to ease her anxiety.

Shane shot her a questioning look. "Did I miss something?"

"You must drive your mother crazy."

"How so?"

"She loves to decorate. I imagine she's asked your opinion a time or two. Tonight, your reaction to every room we've been in has been—" she summoned up her best Shane imitation "—nice." Her laughter swelled. "I'm imagining you doing that to your mother. It's funny."

"Obviously." He stared at her as if he didn't recognize her. But after a moment, his lips relaxed into a smile. "I'll make an effort to be more specific from now on."

"I'm sure your mother will appreciate that."

Deciding they'd spent more than enough time in her bedroom, Brandee headed toward the door. As she passed Shane, he surprised her by catching her arm and using her momentum to swing her up against his body.

"Hey!" she protested even as her traitorous spine softened beneath his palm and her hips relaxed into his.

"Hey, what?" He lowered his lips to her temple and murmured, "I've been waiting too many years to kiss you. Don't you think it's time you put me out of my misery?"

She should've expected he'd make his move as soon as possible, and should've been prepared to deflect his attempt to seduce her. Instead, here she was, up on her toes, flattening her breasts against the hard planes of his chest and aching for that kiss he so obviously intended to take.

"I'm going to need a couple glasses of wine to get me in the mood," she told him, stroking her fingers over his beefy shoulders and into the soft brown waves that spilled over his collar.

"You don't need wine. You have me." His fingers skimmed the sensitive line where her back met her butt, sending lightning skittering along her nerve endings.

She trembled with the effort of keeping still. Seizing her lower lip between her teeth, she contained a groan, but the urge to rub herself all over him was gaining momentum. She needed to decide the smart move here, but couldn't think straight.

Summoning all her willpower, she set her hands on his chest and pushed herself away. "It's not going to happen, Delgado."

Shane raked both hands through his hair, but his grin was unabashed and cocky. "Tonight or ever?"

"Tonight." Lying to him served no purpose.

Given the seesaw of antagonism and attraction, she couldn't imagine them lasting two weeks without tearing each other's clothes off, but she refused to tumble into bed with him right off the bat.

"Fair enough."

Brandee led the way back into the main part of the house and toward the kitchen. When she'd made this wager, she hadn't thought through what sharing her home with Shane would entail. She hadn't lived with anyone since she'd run away from her mother's house twelve years earlier. Realizing she would have to interact with him in such close quarters threw her confidence a curve ball.

"I'm going to open a bottle of wine. Do you want to join me or can I get you something else?" She opened the refrigerator. "I have beer. Or there's whiskey."

"I'll have wine. It wasn't an I-could-use-a-beer sort of day."

Brandee popped the cork on her favorite Shiraz and poured out two glasses. "What sort of day is that?"

"One where I spend it in the saddle or out surveying the pastures." His usually expressive features lost all emotion. And then he gave her a meaningless smile. "You know, ranch work."

"You don't sound as if you're all that keen on ranching."

Because he seemed so much more focused on his real-estate developments, she'd never considered him to be much of a rancher. He gave every appearance of avoiding hard work, so she assumed that he was lazy or entitled.

"Some aspects of it are more interesting than others."

With an hour and a half to kill before dinner, she decided to build a fire in the big stone fireplace out on her covered patio. The cooler weather gave her a great excuse to bundle up and enjoy the outdoor space. She carried the bottle of wine and her glass through the French doors off the dining room.

The days were getting longer, so she didn't have to turn on the overhead lights to find the lighter. The logs were already stacked and waiting for the touch of flame. In a short time a yellow glow spilled over the hearth and illuminated the seating area.

Choosing a seat opposite Shane, Brandee tucked her feet beneath her and sipped her wine. "You do mostly backgrounding at Bullseye, right?"

Backgrounding was the growing of heifers and steers from weanlings to a size where they could enter feedlots for finishing. With nearly fourteen thousand acres, Shane had the space to graze cattle and the skills to buy and sell at the opportune times. He had a far more flexible cattle business than Brandee's, which involved keeping a permanent stock of cows to produce calves that she later sold either to someone like Shane or to other ranches as breeding stock.

"I like the flexibility that approach offers me."

"I can see that."

She'd suffered massive losses after the tornado swept through her property and demolished her operations. She hadn't lost much of her herd, but the dam-

age to her infrastructure had set her way back. And
loss of time as she rebuilt wasn't the sort of thing covered by insurance.

Shane continued, "I don't want to give everything
to the ranch like my father did and end up in an early
grave." Once again, Shane's easy charm vanished beneath a stony expression. But in the instant before that
happened, something like resentment sparked in his
eyes.

This glimpse behind Shane's mask gave Brandee
a flash of insight. For the first time she realized there
might be more to the arrogant Shane Delgado than he
wanted the world to see. And that intrigued her more
than she wanted it to.

She couldn't actually fall for Shane. Her ranch was
at stake. But what if he fell in love with her? Until that
second, Brandee hadn't actually considered the con-
sequences if she won this desperate wager. And then
she shook her head. The thought of Shane falling for
her in two weeks was crazy and irrational. But wasn't
that the way love made a person feel?

Brandee shook her head. She wasn't in danger of
losing her heart to Shane Delgado, only her ranch.

Five

Tossing and turning, his thoughts filled with a woman, wasn't Shane's style, but taking Brandee in his arms for the first time had electrified him. After a nearly sleepless night, he rolled out of bed at five o'clock, heeding her warning that breakfast was at six. The smell of coffee and bacon drew him from the guest suite after a quick shower.

He'd dressed in worn jeans, a long-sleeved shirt and his favorite boots. He intended to show Brandee that while he preferred to run his ranch from his office, he was perfectly capable of putting in a hard day's work.

Shane emerged from the hallway and into the living room. Brandee was working in the kitchen, her blond hair haloed by overhead recessed lighting. With a spatula in one hand and a cup of coffee in the other, she danced and sang to the country song playing softly from her smartphone.

If seeing Brandee relaxed and having fun while she flipped pancakes wasn't enough to short-circuit his equilibrium, the fact that she was wearing a revealing white cotton nightgown beneath a short royal blue silk kimono hit him like a two-by-four to the gut.

Since she hadn't yet noticed him, he had plenty of freedom to gawk at her. Either she'd forgotten he was staying in her guest room or she'd assumed he wasn't going to get up in time for breakfast. Because there was no way she'd let loose like this if she thought he'd catch her.

The soft sway of her breasts beneath the thin cotton mesmerized him, as did the realization that she was a lot more fun than he gave her credit for being. Man, he was in big trouble. If this was a true glimpse of what she could be like off-hours, there was a damn good chance that he'd do exactly what he swore he wouldn't and fall hard. He had to reclaim the upper hand. But at the moment he had no idea how to go about doing that.

"You're into Florida Georgia Line," he said as he approached the large kitchen island and slid onto a barstool. "I would've pegged you as a Faith Hill or Miranda Lambert fan."

"Why, because I'm blond or because I'm a woman?"

He had no good answer. "I guess."

She cocked her head and regarded him with a pitying expression. "The way you think, I'm not surprised you have trouble keeping a woman."

He shrugged. "You got any coffee?"

"Sure." She reached into her cupboard and fetched a mug.

The action caused her nightgown to ride up. Presented with another three inches of smooth skin covering muscular thigh, Shane was having trouble keeping track of the conversation.

"What makes you think I want to keep a woman?"

"Don't you get tired of playing the field?"

"The right woman hasn't come along to make me want to stop."

Brandee bent forward and slid his mug across the concrete counter toward him, offering a scenic view of the sweet curves of her cleavage. In his day he'd seen bigger and better. So why was he dry-mouthed and tongue-tied watching Brandee fixing breakfast?

"What's your definition of the right woman?" She slid the plate of pancakes into the oven to keep them warm.

"She can cook." He really didn't care if she did or not; he just wanted to see Brandee's eyes flash with temper.

She fetched a carton of eggs out of the fridge and held them out to him. "I don't know how to make those disgusting things you eat. So either you eat your eggs scrambled or you make them yourself."

This felt like a challenge. His housekeeper didn't work seven days a week and he knew how to fix eggs. "And she's gotta be great in bed."

"Naturally."

He came around the island as she settled another pan on her six-burner stove and got a flame started under it.

"So as long as she satisfies what lies below your belt,

you're happy?" She cracked two eggs into a bowl and beat them with a whisk.

"Pretty much." Too late Shane remembered that their wager involved her falling in love with him. "And she needs to have a big heart, want kids. She'll be beautiful in a wholesome way, passionate about what she does and, of course, she's gotta be a spitfire."

"That's a big list."

"I guess." And it described Brandee to a tee, except for the part about the kids. He had no idea whether or not she wanted to have children.

"You want kids?"

"Sure." He'd never really thought much about it. "I was an only child. It would've been nice to have a bunch of brothers to get into trouble with."

Her silk kimono dipped off her shoulder as she worked, baring her delicate skin. With her dressed like this and her fine, gold hair tucked behind her ears to reveal tiny silver earrings shaped like flowers, he was having a hard time keeping his mind on the eggs he was supposed to be cracking. His lips would fit perfectly into the hollow of her collarbone. Would she quiver as she'd done the evening before?

Silence reigned in the kitchen until Shane broke it.

"Do you do this every day?" He dropped a bit of butter into his skillet.

"I do this most mornings. Breakfast is the most important meal of the day and trust me, you'll burn this off way before lunch."

Based on the mischief glinting in her eyes, Shane didn't doubt that. What sort of plan had she devised to torment him today? It was probably a morning spent in the saddle cutting out heavies, the cows closest to their due date, and bringing them into the pasture closest to the calving building.

It turned out he was right. Brandee put him up on a stocky buckskin with lightning reflexes. He hadn't cut cows in years and worried that he wouldn't be up to the task, but old skills came back to him readily and he found himself grinning as he worked each calf-heavy cow toward the opening into the next pasture.

"You're not too bad," Brandee said, closing the gate behind the pregnant cow he'd just corralled.

She sat her lean chestnut as if she'd been born in the saddle. Her straw cowboy hat had seen better days. So had her brown chaps and boots. The day had warmed from the lower forties to the midsixties and Brandee had peeled off a flannel-lined denim jacket to reveal a pale blue button-down shirt.

"Thanks." He pulled off his hat and wiped sweat from his brow. "I forgot how much fun that can be."

"A good horse makes all the difference," she said. "Buzz there has been working cows for three years. He likes it. Not all the ones we start take to cutting as well as he has."

Shane patted the buckskin's neck and resettled his hat. "How many more do you have for today?" They'd worked their way through the herd of fifty cows and moved ten of them closer to the calving building.

"I think that's going to be it for now." Brandee guided her horse alongside Shane's.

"How many more are set to go soon?"

"About thirty head in the next week to ten days, I think. Probably another fifteen that are two weeks out."

"And it's not yet peak birthing season. What kind of numbers are you looking at in March?"

With her nearly five thousand acres, Shane guessed she was running around seven hundred cows. That translated to seven hundred births a year. A lot could go wrong.

"It's not as bad as it seems. We split the herd into spring and fall calving. So we're only dropping three to four hundred calves at any one time. This cuts down on the number of short-term ranch hands I need to hire during calving and keeps me from losing a year if a breeding doesn't take."

"It's still a lot of work."

Brandee shrugged. "We do like to keep a pretty close eye on them because if anything can go wrong, chances are it will."

"What are your survival rates?"

"Maybe a little better than average. In the last three years I've only lost four percent of our calves." She looked pretty pleased by that number. "And last fall we only had two that were born dead and only one lost through complications." Her eyes blazed with triumph.

"I imagine it can be hard to lose even one."

"We spend so much time taking care of them every day between feeding, doctoring and pulling calves. It breaks my heart every time something goes wrong. Especially when it's because we didn't get to a cow in time. Or if it's a heifer who doesn't realize she's given birth and doesn't clean up the calf or, worse, wanders off while her wet baby goes hypothermic."

Over the years he'd become so acclimated to Brandee's coolness that he barely recognized the vibrant, intense woman beside him. He was sucker punched by her emotional attachment to the hundreds of babies that got born on her ranch every year.

This really was her passion. And every time he approached her about selling, he'd threatened not just her livelihood but her joy.

"My dad used to go ballistic if that happened," she continued. "I pitied the hand that nodded off during watch and let something go wrong."

"Where's your dad now?"

Her hat dipped, hiding her expression. "He died when I was twelve."

Finding that they had this in common was a surprise. "We both lost our dads too early." Although Shane suspected from Brandee's somber tone that her loss was far keener than his had been. "So, your dad was a rancher, too?"

She shook her head. "A foreman at the Lazy J. But it was his dream to own his own ranch." Her gaze fixed on the horizon. "And for us to run it together."

Shane heard the conviction in her voice and wondered if he should just give up and concede the wager right now. She wasn't going to sell her ranch to him or anyone else. Then he remembered that even if he was faced with a fight he could never win, there was still a good chance she'd sleep with him before the two weeks were up. And wasn't that why he'd accepted the wager in the first place?

* * *

At around two o'clock in the afternoon, Brandee knocked off work so she could grab a nap. It made the long hours to come a little easier if she wasn't dead tired before she got on the horse. Normally during the ninety-day calving season Brandee took one overnight watch per week. She saw no reason to change this routine with Shane staying at her house.

Brandee let herself in the back door and kicked off her boots in the mudroom. Barefoot, she headed into the kitchen for a cheese stick and an apple. Munching contentedly, she savored the house's tranquillity. Sharing her space with Shane was less troublesome than she'd expected, but she'd lived alone a long time and relished the quiet. Shane had a knack for making the air around him crackle with energy.

It didn't help that he smelled like sin and had an adorable yawn, something she'd seen a great deal of him doing these last three days because she'd worked him so hard. In the evenings he had a hard time focusing on his laptop as he answered emails and followed up with issues on The Bellamy job site.

Today, she'd given him the day off to head to the construction site so he could handle whatever problems required him to be there in person. She didn't expect him back until after dinner and decided to indulge in a hot bath before hitting her mattress for a couple hours of shut-eye. It always felt decadent to nap in the afternoon, but she functioned better when rested and reminded herself that she'd hired experienced hands so she didn't have to do everything herself.

Since receiving Maverick's blackmail notice, she hadn't slept well, and though her body was tired, her mind buzzed with frenetic energy. Disrupting her routine further was the amount of time she was spending with Shane. Despite questioning the wisdom of their wager, she realized that having him in her house was a nice change.

Four hours later, Brandee was fixing a quiet dinner for herself of baked chicken and Caesar salad. Shane had a late business meeting and was planning on having dinner in town. He'd only been helping her for three days, but already she could see the impact he was having on her building project at the camp.

He'd gone down to the site and assessed the situation. Last night he'd studied her plans and budget, promising to get her back on track. As much as she hated to admit it, it was good to have someone to partner with. Even if that someone was Shane Delgado and he was only doing it to make her fall in love with him.

There'd been no repeat of him making a play for her despite the way she fixed breakfast every morning in her nightgown. Standing beside him in the kitchen and suffering the bite of sexual attraction, she'd expected something to happen. When nothing had, she'd felt wrung out and cranky. Not that she let him see that. It wouldn't do to let him know that she'd crossed the bridge from it's never going to happen to if it didn't happen soon she'd go mad.

Shane returned to the ranch house as Brandee was getting ready to leave. Her shift wouldn't begin for an hour, but she wanted to get a report on what had happened during the afternoon. As he came in the back door and met up with her in the mudroom, he looked surprised to see her dressed in her work clothes and a warm jacket.

His movements lacked their usual energy as he set his briefcase on the bench. "Are you just getting in?"

"Nope, heading out." She snagged her hat from one of the hooks and set it on her head. "It's my night to watch the cows that are close to calving."

"You're going out by yourself?"

She started to bristle at his question, then decided he wasn't being patronizing, just voicing concern. "I've been doing it for three years by myself. I'll be fine."

"Give me a second to change and I'll come with you."

His offer stunned her. "You must be exhausted." The words slipped out before she considered them.

He turned in the doorway that led to the kitchen and glared at her. "So?"

"I just mean it's a long shift. I spend between four to six hours in the saddle depending on how things go."

"You don't think I'm capable of doing that?"

"I didn't say that." Dealing with his ego was like getting into a ring with a peevish bull. "But you have worked all day and I didn't figure you'd be up for pulling an all-nighter."

"You think I'm soft."

"Not at all." She knew he could handle the work, but was a little surprised he wanted to.

"Then what is it?"

"I just reasoned that you don't…that maybe you

aren't as used to the actual work that goes into ranching."

"That's the same thing."

Brandee regretted stirring the pot. She should have just invited him along and laughed when he fell off his horse at 2:00 a.m. because he couldn't keep his eyes open any longer.

"I don't want to make a big deal about this," she said. "I just thought you might want to get a good night's sleep and start fresh in the morning."

"While you spend the night checking on your herd."

"I took a three-hour nap." His outrage was starting to amuse her. "Okay. You can come with me. I won't say another word."

He growled at her in frustration before striding off. Brandee grabbed a second thermos from her cabinet. Coffee would help keep them warm and awake. To her surprise, Brandee caught herself smiling at the thought of Shane's company tonight. Working together had proven more enjoyable than she'd imagined. She didn't have to keep things professional with Shane the way she did when working with her ranch hands. She'd enjoyed talking strategy and ranch economics with him.

As if he feared she'd head out without him, Shane returned in record time. She handed him a scarf and watched in silence as he stepped into his work boots.

"Ready?" she prompted as he stood.

"Yes."

"Do you want to take separate vehicles? That way if you get…" She trailed off as his scowl returned. "Fine."

Irritation radiated from him the whole drive down

to the ranch buildings. In the barn, she chatted with her foreman, Jimmy, to see how the afternoon had gone. H545 had dropped her calf without any problems.

"A steer," he said, sipping at the coffee Brandee had just made.

"That makes it fifty-five steers and fifty-two heifers." While the ratio of boys to girls was usually fifty-fifty, it was always nice when more steers were born because they grew faster and weighed more than the girls. "Anyone we need to keep an eye on tonight?"

"H729 was moving around like her labor was starting. She's a week late and if you remember she had some problems last year, so you might want to make sure things are going smoothly with her."

"Will do. Thanks, Jimmy."

The moon was up, casting silvery light across the grass when Shane and Brandee rode into the pasture. The pregnant cows stood or lay in clusters. A couple moved about in a lazy manner. H729 was easy to spot. She was huge and had isolated herself. Brandee pointed her out.

"She's doing some tail wringing, which means she's feeling contractions. I don't think she'll go tonight, but you can never tell."

"How often do they surprise you?"

"More often than I'd like to admit. And that drives me crazy because there's nothing wrong with nearly eighty percent of the calves we lose at birth. Most of the time they suffocate because they're breeched or because it's a first-calf heifer and she gets too tired to finish pushing out the calf."

"How often do you have to assist?"

"On nights like this it's pretty rare." The temperature was hovering in the low forties; compared to a couple weeks earlier, it almost felt balmy. "It's when we get storms and freezing rain that we have our hands full with the newborns."

Shane yawned and rubbed his eyes. Brandee glanced his way to assess his fatigue and lingered to admire his great bone structure and sexy mouth. It was an interesting face, one she never grew tired of staring at. Not a perfect face—she wasn't into that, too boring—but one with character.

"What?" he snapped, never taking his focus off the cows. Despite the shadow cast by the brim of his hat, Brandee could see that Shane's jaw was set.

"I was just thinking it was nice to have your company tonight."

For the briefest of moments his lips relaxed. "I'm glad to be here."

She knew that showing she felt sorry for him would only heighten his annoyance. Big strong men like Shane did not admit to weakness of any kind. And she rather liked him the better for gritting his teeth and sticking with it.

"That being said, you can take my truck and head back if you want. I don't think much of anything is going to happen tonight."

"I don't like the idea of you being alone out here."

"I've been doing this since I was ten years old."

"Not alone."

"No. With my dad. On the weekends, he used to let me ride the late-night watch with him."

"What did your mom say about that?"

"Nothing. She didn't live with us."

Shane took a second to digest that. "They divorced?"

"Never married."

"How come you lived with your dad and not your mom?"

Insulated by her father's unconditional love, Brandee had never noticed her mother's absence. "She didn't want me."

It wasn't a plea for sympathy, but a statement of fact. Most people would have said her mother was a bad parent or uttered some banality about how they were sure that wasn't true.

Shane shrugged. "You are kind of a pain."

He would never know how much she appreciated this tactic. Shane might come off as a glib charmer, but the way he watched her now showed he had a keen instinct for people.

"Yes," Brandee drawled. "She mentioned that often after my dad died and I had to go live with her."

Judging from his narrowed eyes, he wasn't buying her casual posture and nonchalant manner. "Obviously she wasn't interested in being a parent," he said.

Brandee loosed a huge sigh and an even bigger confession. "I was the biggest mistake she ever made."

Six

Shane's exhaustion dwindled as Brandee spoke of her mother. Although he'd grown up with both parents, his father's endless disappointment made Shane sympathetic of Brandee for the resentment her mother had displayed.

"Why do you say that?"

"She gave birth to me and handed me over to my dad, then walked out of the hospital and never looked back. After my dad died and the social worker contacted my mom, I was really surprised when she took me in. I think she wanted to get her hands on the money that my dad left me. He'd saved about fifty thousand toward the down payment on his own ranch. She went through it in six months."

"And you got nothing?"

"Not a penny."

"So your father died when you were twelve and your mother spent your inheritance."

"That about sums it up." Brandee spoke matter-of-factly, but Shane couldn't imagine her taking it all in stride. No child grew up thinking it was okay when a parent abandoned them. This must have been what led to Brandee erecting her impenetrable walls. And now Shane was faced with an impossible task. The terms of her wager made much more sense. There was no way he was going to get her to fall for him.

After a slow circle of the pasture, Brandee declared it was quiet enough that they could return to the barn. Leaving the horses saddled and tied up, they grabbed some coffee and settled in the ranch office. While Brandee looked over her herd data, updated her birth statistics and considered her spring-breeding program, Shane used the time to research her.

"You started a fashion line?" He turned his phone so the screen faced her.

She regarded the image of herself modeling a crocheted halter, lace-edged scarf and headband. "A girl's got to pay the bills."

"When you were eighteen?"

"Actually, I was seventeen. I fudged my age. You have to be eighteen to open a business account at the bank and sell online."

"From these news articles, it looks like you did extremely well."

"Who knew there was such a huge hole in the mar-

ket for bohemian-style fashion and accessories." Her
wry smile hid a wealth of pride in her accomplishment.

"You built up the business and sold it for a huge
profit."

"So that I could buy Hope Springs Ranch."

He regarded her with interest. "Obviously the fashion line was a moneymaker. Why not do both?"

"Because my dream was this ranch. And the company was more than a full-time job. I couldn't possibly
keep up with both." She picked up her hat and stood.
"We should do another sweep."

Back in the saddle, facing an icy wind blowing
across the flat pasture, Shane considered the woman
riding beside him. The photos of her modeling her
clothing line had shown someone much more care-
free and happy than she'd ever appeared to him. Why,
if there'd been such good money to be made running
a fashion company, had she chosen the backbreaking
work of running a ranch?

Was it because she'd been trying to continue her father's legacy, molded by him to wake up early, put in
a long day and take satisfaction in each calf that survived? From the way she talked about her dad, Shane
bet there'd been laughter at the end of each day and a
love as wide as the Texas sky.

He envied her.

"Is that the cow you were watching earlier?" He
pointed out an animal in the distance that had just
lain down.

"Maybe. Let's double-check."

When they arrived, they left their horses and approached the cow on foot. Judging from the way her sides were straining, she was deep in labor.

It struck Shane that despite spending his entire life on a ranch, he'd only witnessed a few births, and those had been horses not cows. He took his cue from Brandee. She stood with her weight evenly placed, her gloved hands bracketing her hips. Although her eyes were intent, her manner displayed no concern.

"Look," she said as they circled around to the cow's rear end. "You can see the water sack."

Sure enough, with the moon high in the sky there was enough light for Shane to pick out the opaque sack that contained the calf. He hadn't come out tonight expecting excitement of this sort.

"What did you expect?" It was as if she'd read his mind.

"Frankly I was thinking we'd be riding around out here while you kept me at arm's length with tales of your brokenhearted ex-lovers."

With her arms crossed over her chest, she pivoted around to face him, laboring cow forgotten.

"My brokenhearted what?"

"I don't know," he replied somewhat shortly. "I'm tired and just saying whatever pops into my mind."

"Why would you be thinking about my broken-hearted ex-lovers?"

"Are you sure she's doing okay?" He indicated the straining cow, hoping to distract Brandee with something important.

Unfortunately it seemed as if both females were happy letting nature take its course. Brandee continued to regard him like a detective interviewing a prime suspect she knew was lying.

"What makes you think that any of my lovers are brokenhearted?"

"I don't. Not really." In truth he hadn't given much thought to her dating anyone.

Well, that wasn't exactly true. To the best of his knowledge she hadn't dated anyone since moving to Royal. And despite the womanly curves that filled out her snug denim, she always struck him as a tomboy. Somehow he'd gotten it into his head that he was the only one who might've been attracted to her.

"So which is it?"

"Is that a hoof?"

His attempt to distract her lasted as long as it took for her to glance over at the cow and notice that a pair of hooves had emerged.

"Yes." And just like that she was back staring at him again. "Do I strike you as the sort of woman who uses men and casts them aside?"

"No."

"So why would you think I would end my relationships in such a way that I would hurt someone?"

Shane recognized that he'd tapped into something complicated with his offhand remark and sought to defuse her irritation with a charming smile. "You should be flattered that I thought you would be so desirable that no one would ever want to break up with you."

"So you think I'm susceptible to flattery?"

He was in so deep he would need a hundred feet of rope to climb out of the hole he'd dug. What had happened to the silver-tongued glibness she liked to accuse him of having?

"Is she supposed to stand up like that?"

"Sometimes they need to walk around a bit." This time Brandee didn't spare the cow even a fraction of her attention. "She may be up and down several times."

"I think our arguing is upsetting her," he said, hoping concern for the cow would convince Brandee to give up the conversation.

"We're not arguing," she corrected him, her voice light and unconcerned. "We're discussing your opinion of me. And you're explaining why you assume I'd be the one to end a relationship. Instead of the other way around."

At first he grappled with why he'd said what he had. But beneath her steady gaze, he found his answer. "I think you have a hard time finding anyone who can match up to your father."

She obviously hadn't expected him to deliver such a blunt, to-the-point answer. Her eyes fell away and she stared at the ground. In the silence that followed, Shane worried that he'd struck too close to home.

Brandee turned so she was once again facing the cow. The brim of her hat cast a shadow over her features, making her expression unreadable. Despite her silence, Shane didn't sense she was angry. Her mood was more contemplative than irritated.

"I never set out to hurt anyone," she said, her voice so soft he almost missed the words. "I'm just not good girlfriend material."

Was that her way of warning him off? If so, she'd

have to work a lot harder. "That's something else we have in common. I've been told I'm not good boyfriend material, either."

Now both of them were staring at the cow. She took several steps before coming to a halt as another spasm swept over her. It seemed as if this would expel the calf, but no more of the baby appeared.

"Is this normal?" Shane asked. "It seems like she can't get it out."

"We should see good progress in the next thirty minutes or so. If we don't see the nose and face by then, there might be something wrong."

Shane was surprised at the way his stomach knotted with anxiety. Only by glancing at Brandee's calm posture did he keep from voicing his concern again.

"How do you do this?"

"I have around seven hundred cows being bred over two seasons. While I never take anything for granted, watching that many births gives you a pretty good feel for how things are going."

"Your business is a lot more complicated than mine." And offered a lot more potential for heartbreak.

He certainly wasn't standing in his field at three o'clock in the morning waiting for new calves to be brought into the world. He bought eight-month-old, newly weaned steers and heifers and sent them out into his pastures to grow up. Unless he was judging the market for the best time to sell, he rarely thought about his livestock.

"Not necessarily more complicated," Brandee said. "You have to consider the market when you buy and sell and the best way to manage your pastures to optimize grazing. There are so many variables that depend on how much rain we get and the price of feed if the pastures aren't flourishing."

"But you have all that to worry about and you have to manage when you're breeding and optimize your crosses to get the strongest calves possible. And then there's the problem of losing livestock to accidents and predators."

While he'd been speaking, the cow had once again lain down. The calf's nose appeared, followed by a face. Shane stared as she began to push in earnest.

"She's really straining," he said. "This is all still normal?"

"She needs to push out the shoulders and this is really hard. But she's doing fine."

Shane had the urge to lean his body into Brandee's and absorb some of her tranquillity. Something about the quiet night and the miracle playing out before them made him want to connect with her. But he kept his distance, not wanting to disturb the fragile camaraderie between them.

Just when Shane thought the whole thing was over, the cow got to her feet again and he groaned. Brandee shot him an amused grin.

"It's okay. Sometimes they like finishing the birthing process standing up."

He watched as the cow got to her feet, her baby dangling halfway out of her. This time Shane didn't resist the urge for contact. He reached out and grabbed Brandee's hand. He'd left his gloves behind on this second sweep and wished Brandee had done the same. But despite the worn leather barrier between them, he reveled in the way her fingers curved against his.

After a few deep, fortifying breaths, the cow gave one last mighty push and the calf fell to the grass with a thud. Shane winced and Brandee laughed.

"See, I told you it was going to be okay," Brandee said as the cow turned around and began nudging the calf while making soft, encouraging grunts.

A moment later she swept her long tongue over her sodden baby, clearing fluid from the calf's coat. The calf began to breathe and the cow kept up her zealous cleaning. Brandee leaned a little of her weight against Shane's arm.

That was when Shane realized they were still holding hands. "Damn," he muttered, unsure which had a bigger impact, the calf being born or the simple pleasure of Brandee's hand in his.

He hadn't answered the question before she lifted up on tiptoes and kissed him.

Being bathed in moonlight and surrounded by the sleepy cows seemed like an ideal moment to surrender to the emotions running deep and untamed through Brandee's body. At first Shane's lips were stiff with surprise and Brandee cursed. What had she been thinking? There was no romance to be found in a cold, windswept pasture. But as she began her retreat, Shane threw an arm around her waist and yanked her hard against his body. His lips softened and coaxed a sigh of relief from her lungs.

She wrapped her arms around his neck and let him sweep her into a rushing stream of longing. The mouth that devoured her with such abandon lacked the persuasive touch she'd expected a charmer like Shane to wield. It almost seemed as if he was as surprised as she.

Of course, there was no way that could be the case. His reasons for being at her ranch were as self-serving as hers had been for inviting him. Each of them wanted to win their wager. She'd intended to do whatever it took to get Shane to fall in love with her. Her dire situation made that a necessity. But he'd been pestering her for years to sell and she was sure he'd pull out every weapon in his arsenal to get her to fall for him.

This last thought dumped cold water on her libido. She broke off the kiss and through the blood roaring in her ears heard the measured impact of approaching hooves all around them. It wasn't unusual for the most dominant cows in the herd to visit the newborn. Half a dozen cows had approached.

"He's looking around," she said, indicating the new calf. "Soon he'll be trying to get up."

Usually a calf was on its feet and nursing within the first hour of being born. Brandee would have to make sure her ranch hands kept an eye on him for the next twelve hours to make sure he got a good suckle. And they would need to get him ear-tagged and weighed first thing. The calves were docile and trusting the first day. After that they grew much more difficult to catch.

Brandee stepped away from Shane and immediately missed their combined body heat. "I think it's okay to head back."

"I'm glad I came out tonight," Shane said as they rode back toward the horse barn. A quick sweep of the pasture had shown nothing else of interest.

"You're welcome to participate in night duty anytime."

"How often do you pull a shift?"

"Once a week."

"You don't have to."

"No." But how did she explain that sitting on a horse in the middle of the night, surrounded by her pregnant cows, she felt as if everything was perfect in her world? "But when I'm out here I think about my dad smiling down and I know he'd be happy with me."

She didn't talk about her dad all that much to anyone. But because of Shane's awestruck reaction to tonight's calving, she was feeling sentimental.

"Happy because you're doing what he wanted?"

"Yes."

"How about what you want?"

"It's the same thing." Brandee's buoyant mood suddenly drooped like a thirsty flower. "Being a rancher is all I ever wanted to do."

"And yet you started a fashion business instead of coming back to find work as a ranch hand. You couldn't know that what you were doing with your clothing line would make you rich."

"No." She'd never really thought about why she'd chosen waitressing and creating clothing and accessories after running away from her mother's house over getting work on a ranch. "I guess I wasn't sure anyone would take me serious as a ranch hand." And it was a job dominated by men.

"You might be right."

When they arrived at the barn, this time Brandee insisted Shane take her truck back to the ranch house. She wasn't going to finish up work until much later. He seemed reluctant, but in the end he agreed.

The instant the truck's taillights disappeared down the driveway, Brandee was struck by a ridiculous feeling of loneliness. She turned on the computer and recorded the ranch's newest addition. Then, hiding a yawn behind her hand, she made her way to the barn where they housed cows and calves that needed more attention.

Cayenne was a week old. A couple days ago a ranch hand had noticed her hanging out on her own by the hay, abandoned by her mother. At this age it didn't take long for a calf to slide downhill, so it paid to be vigilant. Jimmy had brought her in and the guys had tended to a cut on her hind left hoof.

They'd given her a bottle with some electrolytes and a painkiller and the calf had turned around in two days. She was a feisty thing and it made Brandee glad to see the way she charged toward the half wall as if she intended to smash through it. At the very last second she wheeled away, bucking and kicking her way around the edge of the enclosure.

Brandee leaned her arms on the wood and spent a few minutes watching the calf, wondering if the mother would take back her daughter when they were reunited. Sometimes a cow just wasn't much of a mother and when that happened they'd load her up and take her to the sales barn. No reason to feed an unproductive cow.

Talking about being abandoned by her own mother wasn't something Brandee normally did, but it had proven easy to tell Shane. So easy that she'd also divulged the theft of her inheritance, something she'd only ever told to one other person, her best friend, Chelsea.

In the aftermath of the conversation, she'd felt exposed and edgy. It was partially why she'd picked a fight with him about his "brokenhearted ex-lovers" comment. She'd wanted to bring antagonism back into their interaction. Fighting with him put her back on solid ground, kept her from worrying that he'd see her as weak and her past hurts as exploitable.

At the same time his offhand comment had unknowingly touched a nerve. She'd asked if he saw her as the sort of woman who'd use a man and cast him aside. Yet she'd done it before and had barely hesitated before deciding to do so with Shane. She was going to make him fall for her and trick him into giving up his legal claim to Hope Springs Ranch. What sort of a terrible person did that make her?

Reminding herself that he intended to take the ranch didn't make her feel better about what she was doing. He had no clue about the enormity of their wager. Keeping him in the dark wasn't fair or right. Yet, if he discovered the truth, she stood to lose everything.

As during her teen years living with her mother, she was in pure survival mode. It was the only thing that kept her conscience from hamstringing her. She didn't enjoy what she was doing. It was necessary to protect what belonged to her and keep herself safe. Like a cat cornered by a big dog, she would play as dirty as it took to win free and clear.

Several hours later, after one final sweep of the pasture, she turned the watch over to her ranch hands and had one of them drop her off at home. She probably could've walked the quarter-mile-long driveway to her house, but the emotional night had taken a toll on her body as well as her spirit.

The smell of bacon hit her as she entered the back door and her stomach groaned in delight. With loud country music spilling from the recessed speakers above her kitchen and living room, she was able to drop her boots in the mudroom and hang up her coat and hat, then sneak through the doorway to catch a glimpse of Shane without him being aware.

Her heart did a strange sort of hiccup in her chest at the sight of him clad in baggy pajama bottoms, a pale blue T-shirt riding his chest and abs like a second skin. She gulped at the thought of running her hands beneath the cotton and finding the silky, warm texture beneath. While the man might be a piece of work, his body was a work of art.

"Hey." She spoke the word softly, but he heard.

His gaze shifted toward her and the slow smile that curved his lips gave her nerve endings a delicious jolt. She had to hold on to the door frame while her knees returned to a solid state capable of supporting her. He was definitely working the sexy-roommate angle for all it was worth. She'd better up her game.

"I'm making breakfast just the way you like it." He held up the skillet and showed her the eggs he'd scrambled. "And there's French toast, bacon and coffee."

Damn. And he could cook, too. Conscious of her disheveled hair and the distinctive fragrance of horse and barn that clung to her clothes, Brandee debated slinking off to grab a quick shower or just owning these badges of hard work.

"It all sounds great." Her stomach growled loudly enough to be heard and Shane's eyebrows went up.

"Let me make you a plate," he said, laughter dancing at the edges of his voice. "Here's a cup of coffee. Go sit down before you fall over."

That he'd misinterpreted why she was leaning against the doorway was just fine with Brandee. She accepted the coffee and made her way toward the bar stools that lined her kitchen island. Unconcerned about whether the caffeine zap would keep her awake, she gladly sipped the dark, rich brew.

"It's decaf," he remarked, sliding a plate toward her and then turning back to the stove to fill one for himself. "I figured you'd grab a couple hours before heading out again."

"Thanks," she mumbled around a mouthful of French toast. "And thanks for breakfast. You didn't have to."

His broad shoulders lifted in a lazy shrug. "I slept a few hours and thought you'd be hungry. How's the new calf?"

"On my last circuit he was enjoying his first meal."

"Great to hear." Shane slid into the seat beside her and set his plate down. His bare feet found the rungs of her chair, casually invading her space. "Thanks for letting me tag along last night." He peered at her for a long moment before picking up his fork and turning his attention to breakfast.

"Sure."

As they ate in companionable silence, Brandee found her concern growing by the minute. The night's shared experience and his thoughtfulness in having breakfast ready for her were causing a shift in her impression of him. For years she'd thought of Shane as an egomaniac focused solely on making money. Tonight she'd seen his softer side, and the hint of vulnerability made him attractive to her in a different way.

A more dangerous way.

She had to stay focused on her objective and not give in to the emotions tugging at her. Letting him capture her heart was a mistake. One that meant she would lose everything. Her home. Her livelihood. And worst of all, her self-respect. Because falling for a man who wouldn't return her love was really stupid and she'd been many things, but never that.

Seven

It was almost six o'clock in the evening when Shane returned from checking on the building site at Brandee's teen camp. As he entered the house through the back door, the most delicious scents stopped him dead in his tracks. He breathed in the rich scent of beef and red wine as he stripped off his coat and muddy boots. In stockinged feet, he entered the kitchen, where Brandee's housekeeper stood at the stove, stirring something in a saucepan.

"What smells so amazing?"

"Dinner," May responded with a cheeky grin and a twinkle in her bright blue eyes.

The fiftysomething woman had rosy cheeks even when she wasn't standing over the stove. She fussed over Brandee like a fond aunt rather than a housekeeper and treated Shane as if he was the best thing that had ever happened to her employer.

"What are we having?"

"Beef Wellington with red potatoes and asparagus."

Shane's mouth began to water. "What's the occasion?"

"Valentine's Day." May pointed toward the dining table, where china and silverware had been laid. There were white tapers in crystal holders and faceted goblets awaiting wine. "You forgot?"

Eyeing the romantic scene, Shane's heart thumped erratically. What special hell was he in for tonight?

"I've been a little preoccupied," he muttered.

Between helping out at Hope Springs, keeping an eye on the construction at The Bellamy and popping in at Bullseye to make sure all was running smoothly, he hadn't had five minutes to spare. Now he was kicking himself for missing this opportunity to capitalize on the most romantic day of the year to sweep Brandee off her feet.

Obviously she hadn't made the same mistake.

May shook her head as if Shane had just proven what was wrong with the entire male sex. "Well, it's too late to do anything about it now. Dinner's in half an hour." She arched her eyebrows at his mud-splattered jeans.

Catching her meaning, Shane headed for his shower. Fifteen minutes later, he'd washed off the day's exertions and dressed in clean clothes. He emerged from his bedroom, tugging up the sleeves of his gray sweater.

Black jeans and a pair of flip-flops completed his casual look.

Brandee was peering into her wine fridge as he approached. She turned at his greeting and smiled in genuine pleasure. "How was your day?"

"Good. Productive." It was a casual exchange, lacking the push and pull of sexual attraction that typified their usual interaction. Time to step up his game. "Did May head home?"

"Yes. She and Tim were going out for a romantic dinner."

"Because it's Valentine's Day. I forgot all about it."

"So did I." Brandee selected a bottle and set it on the counter. With her long golden hair cascading over the shoulders of her filmy top, she looked like a cross between a sexy angel and the girl next door. White cotton shorts edged in peekaboo lace rode low on her hips and bared her sensational, well-toned thighs. "Can you open this while I fetch the glasses? The corkscrew is in the drawer to your right."

"I guess neither one of us buys into all the romantic mumbo jumbo," he muttered.

He should've been relieved that the fancy dinner and beautifully set dining table hadn't been Brandee's idea. It meant that she hadn't set out to prey on his libido. But that didn't mean the danger had passed.

"Or we're just cynical about love." She gazed at him from beneath her long eyelashes.

Shane finished opening the bottle and set it aside to breathe. He worked the cork off the corkscrew, letting the task absorb his full attention. "Do you ever wonder if you're built for a long-term relationship?" He recognized it was a strange question to ask a woman, but he suspected Brandee wouldn't be insulted.

"All the time." She moved past him as the timer on the stove sounded. Apparently this was her signal to remove the beef Wellington from the oven. "I don't make my personal life a priority. Chelsea's on me all the time about it."

"My mom gives me the same sort of lectures. I think she wants grandchildren." And he was getting to an age where he needed to decide kids or no kids. At thirty-five he wasn't over the hill by any means, but he didn't want to be in his forties and starting a family.

"I imagine she's feeling pretty hopeless about the possibility."

"Because I haven't met anyone that makes me want to settle down?"

Brandee shook her head. "I can't imagine any woman being more important to you than your freedom."

And she was right. His bachelor status suited him. Having fun. Keeping things casual. Bolting at the first sign of commitment. He liked keeping his options open. And what was wrong with that?

"And what about you, Miss Independent? Are you trying to tell me you're any more eager to share your life with someone? You use your commitment to this ranch and your teen camp to keep everyone at bay. What are you afraid of?"

"Who says I'm afraid?"

Bold words, but he'd seen the shadows that lingered in her eyes when she talked about her mother's abandonment. She might deny it, but there was no question in Shane's mind that Brandee's psyche had taken a hit.

"It's none of my business. Forget I said anything." Shane sensed that if he pursued the issue he would only end up annoying her and that was not how he wanted the evening to go.

"Why don't you pour the wine while I get food on the plates." From her tone, she was obviously content to drop the topic.

Ten minutes later they sat down to the meal May had prepared. Shane kept the conversation fixed on the progress she was making at her teen camp. It was a subject near and dear to her heart, and helping her with the project was sure to endear him to her. Was it manipulative? Sure. But he wanted to buy her property. That's why he'd accepted the bet and moved in.

Shane ignored a tug at his conscience and reminded himself that Brandee was working just as hard as he was to make him fall for her. He grinned. She just didn't realize that she'd lost before she even started.

"This weekend I'm hosting a teen experience with some of the high school kids," Brandee said. "Megan Maguire from Royal Safe Haven is bringing several of her rescue dogs to the ranch for the teens to work with. Chelsea is coming to help out. I could use a couple more adult volunteers." She regarded him pointedly.

The last thing he wanted to do was spend a day chaperoning a bunch of hormonally charged kids, but he had a wager to win and since he'd dropped the ball for Valentine's Day, he could probably pick up some bonus points by helping her out with this.

"Sure, why not." It wasn't the most enthusiastic response, but he hoped she'd be pleased he'd agreed so readily.

"And maybe you could see if Gabe is interested, as well?"

If it made Brandee go all lovey-dovey for him, Shane would do as much arm-twisting as it took to get his best friend on board. "I'll check with him. I'm sure it won't be a problem."

After putting away the leftovers and settling the dirty dishes in the dishwasher, Brandee suggested they move out to the patio to enjoy an after-dinner scotch. This time, instead of taking the sofa opposite him, she settled onto the cushion right beside him and tucked her feet beneath her.

While the fire crackled and flickered, Shane sipped his drink and, warmed by alcohol, flame and desire, listened while Brandee told him about the struggling calf they'd saved and reunited with her mother today. He told himself that when Brandee leaned into him as she shared her tale she was only acting. Still, it was all Shane could do to keep from pulling her onto his lap and stealing a kiss or two.

"You know, it is Valentine's Day," she murmured, tilting her head to an adorable angle and regarding him from beneath her long lashes.

With her gaze fixed on his lips, Shane quelled the impulses turning his insides into raw need. She was playing him. He knew it and she knew he knew it. For the moment he was willing to concede she had the upper hand. What man presented with an enticing package of sweet and spicy femininity would be capable of resisting?

"Yes, it is," he replied, not daring to sip from the tumbler of scotch lest she see the slight tremble in his hand.

"A day devoted to lovers."

Shane decided to follow her lead and see where it took him. "And romance."

"I think both of us know what's inevitable."

"That you and I get together?" To his credit he didn't sound as hopeful as he felt.

"Exactly." She leaned forward to kiss him. Her lips, whether by design or intent, grazed his cheek instead. Her breath smelled of chocolate and scotch, sending blood scorching through his veins. "I've been thinking about you a lot."

Her husky murmur made his nerve endings shiver. He gripped the glass tumbler hard enough to shatter it. "Me, too. I lay in bed at night and imagine you're with me. Your long hair splayed on my pillow." Thighs parted in welcome. Skin flushed with desire. "You're smiling up at me. Excited by all the incredible things I'm doing to you."

From deep in her throat came a sexy hum. "Funny." Her fingertips traced circles on the back of his neck before soothing their way into his hair. "I always picture myself on top. Your hands on my breasts as I ride you."

Shane winced as his erection suddenly pressed hard against his zipper. "You drive me crazy," he murmured. "You know that, right?"

He set down his drink with a deliberate movement

before cupping her head. She didn't resist as he pulled her close enough to kiss. Her lashes fluttered downward, lips arching into a dreamy smile.

Their breath mingled. Shane drew out the moment. Her soft breasts settled against his chest and he half closed his eyes to better savor the sensation. This wouldn't be their first kiss, but that didn't make it any less momentous. Tonight they weren't in the middle of a pasture surrounded by cows. This time, the only thing standing in the way of seeing this kiss through to the end was if she actually felt something for him.

Was that what made him hesitate? Worry over her emotional state? Or was he more concerned about his own?

"Let's go inside," she suggested, shifting her legs off the couch and taking his hand. Her expression was unreadable as she got to her feet and tugged at him. "I have a wonderful idea about how we can spend the rest of the evening."

The instant they stepped away from the raging fire, Brandee shivered as the cool February air struck her bare skin. She'd dressed to show off a ridiculous amount of flesh in an effort to throw Shane off his game. Naturally her ploy had worked, but as they crossed the brick patio, she wished she hadn't left the throw behind. Despite how readily Shane had taken her up on her offer, she was feeling incredibly uncertain and exposed.

In slow stages during their romantic dinner, her plan to methodically seduce him had gone awry. She blamed it on the man's irresistible charm and the way he'd listened to her talk about the calf and her camp. He hadn't waited in polite silence for her to conclude her explanation about the program she and Megan Maguire had devised to teach the teenagers about patience and responsibility. No, he'd asked great questions and seemed genuinely impressed by the scope of her project.

But the pivotal moment had come when she saw a flash of sympathy in his eyes. She'd been talking about one particular boy whose dad had bullied him into joining the football team when all the kid wanted to do was play guitar and write music. Something about the story had struck home with Shane and for several seconds he'd withdrawn like a hermit crab confronted by something unpleasant. She realized they were alike in so many ways, each burying past hurts beneath a veneer of confidence, keeping the world at bay to keep their sadness hidden.

As they neared the house, a brief skirmish ensued. Shane seemed to expect that Brandee would want their first encounter to be in her bedroom. That was not going to happen. She'd invited him into the space once and it had been a huge mistake. Her bedroom was her sanctuary, the place she could be herself and drop her guard. She didn't want to be vulnerable in front of Shane. Seeing her true self would give him an edge that she couldn't afford.

"Let's try out the shower in your suite," she suggested, taking his hand in both of hers and drawing him toward the sliding glass door that led to his bedroom. "I had such fun designing the space and haven't ever tried it out."

"The rain shower system is pretty fantastic."

The four recessed showerheads in the ceiling and integrated chromotherapy with mood-enhancing colored lighting sequences were ridiculous indulgences, but Brandee had thought her grandmother would get a kick out of it and had been right.

Shane guided her through the bedroom. His hand on the small of her back was hot through the semisheer material of her blouse and Brandee burned. How was it possible that the man who stood poised to take everything from her could be the one who whipped her passions into such a frenzy? They hadn't even kissed and her loins ached for his possession. She shuddered at the image of what was to come, a little frightened by how badly she wanted it.

While Shane used the keypad to start the shower, Brandee gulped in a huge breath and fought panic. How was she supposed to pretend like this was just a simple sexual encounter when each heartbeat made her chest hurt? Every inch of her body hummed with longing. She was so wound up that she was ready to go off the instant he put his hands on her.

Shane picked that second to turn around. Whatever he saw in her expression caused his nostrils to flare and his eyes to narrow. Her nerve collapsed. Brandee backed up a step, moving fully clothed into the shower spray. She blinked in surprise as the warm water raced down her face. Shane didn't hesitate before joining her.

As he circled her waist, drawing her against his

hard planes, Brandee slammed the door on her emotions and surrendered to the pleasure of Shane's touch. She quested her fingers beneath his sweater, stripping the sodden cotton over his head. The skin she revealed stretched over taut muscle and sculpted bone, making her groan in appreciation.

Almost tentatively she reached out to run her palm across one broad shoulder. His biceps flexed as he slid his hands over her rib cage, thumbs whisking along the outer curves of her breasts. She shuddered at the glancing contact and trembled as he licked water from her throat. Hunger built inside her while her breath came in ragged pants.

The water rendered her clothes nearly transparent, but Shane's gaze remained locked on her face. He appeared more interested in discovering her by touch. His fingertips skimmed her arms, shoulders and back with tantalizing curiosity. If she could catch her breath, she might have protested that she needed his hands on her bare skin. An insistent pressure bloomed between her thighs. She felt Shane's own arousal pressing hard against her belly. Why was he making her wait?

In the end she took matters into her own hands and stripped off her blouse. It clung to her skin, resisting all effort to bare herself to his touch. Above the sound of the rain shower, she heard a seam give, but she didn't care. She flung the garment aside. It landed in the corner with a plop. At last she stood before him, clad only in her white lace shorts and bra. And waited.

Shane's breath was as unsteady as hers as he slipped his fingers beneath her narrow bra straps and eased them off her shoulders. Holding her gaze with his, he trailed the tips of his fingers along the lace edge where it met her skin. Brandee's trembling grew worse. She reached behind her and unfastened the hooks. The bra slid to the floor and she seized Shane's hands, moving his palms over her breasts.

Together they shifted until Brandee felt smooth tile against her back. Trapped between the wall and Shane's strong body, hunger exploded in her loins. She wrapped one leg around Shane's hip and draped her arms over his shoulders. At long last he took the kiss she so desperately wanted to give and his tongue plunged into her mouth in feverish demand.

Brandee thrilled to his passion and gave back in equal measures. The kiss seemed to go on forever while water poured over his shoulders and ran between their bodies. Shane's hands were everywhere, cupping her breasts, roaming over her butt, slipping over her abdomen to the waistband of her shorts.

Unlike his jeans with their button and zipper, her lacy cotton shorts were held in place by a satin ribbon. He had the bow loosened and the material riding down her legs in seconds. A murmur of pleasure slipped from his lips when he discovered her satin thong, but it was soon following her shorts to the shower floor.

Naked before him, Brandee quaked. In the early years of her fashion line, she'd modeled all the clothes up for sale at her online store, even the lingerie. She'd lost all modesty about her body. Or so she'd thought.

Shane stepped back and took his time staring at her.

She pressed her palms against the tile wall to keep from covering herself, but it wasn't her lack of clothing that left her feeling exposed. Rather, it was the need for him to find her desirable.

"You are so damned beautiful," he said, sweeping water from his face and hair. His lips moved into a predatory smile. "And all mine."

She hadn't expected such a provocative claim and hid her delight behind flirtation. Setting her hands on her hips, she shot him a saucy grin. "Why don't you slip out of those wet jeans and come get me?"

Without releasing her from the grip of his intense gaze, he popped the button on his jeans and unzipped the zipper. He peeled off black denim and underwear. Brandee's breath lodged in her throat at what was revealed.

The man was more gorgeous than she'd imagined. Broad shoulders tapered into washboard abs. His thighs were corded with muscle. The jut of his erection made her glad she still had the wall at her back because her muscles weakened at the sight of so much raw masculinity.

"Come here." She had no idea how her voice could sound so sexy and calm when her entire being was crazy out of control.

He returned to her without hesitation and captured both her hands, pinning them against the wall on either side of her head. His erection pressing against her belly, he lowered his head and kissed her, deep and demanding. Brandee yielded her mouth and surrendered all control.

This was what she needed. A chance to let go and trust. He was in charge, and in this moment, she was okay with that.

When he freed her hands, she put her arms around his neck, needing the support as he stepped between her feet, widening her stance. His teeth grazed her throat while his hand slid between their bodies and found her more than ready for his possession.

She moaned feverishly as he slid a finger inside her, the heel of his palm grazing the over-stimulated knot of nerves. Gasping, she writhed against his hand while hunger built. She needed him inside her, pumping hard, driving her relentlessly into a massive orgasm.

It was hard to concentrate as he masterfully drove her forward into her climax, but Brandee retained enough of her faculties to offer him a small taste of the torment he was inflicting upon her. She cupped her palm over the head of his erection and felt him shudder.

"Jeez" was all he could manage between clenched teeth.

"We need a condom." She rode his length up and down with her hand, learning the texture and shape of him. "Now."

"Yes."

"Where?"

"Jeans."

"You're prepared." A bubble of amusement gave

her enough breathing room to stave off the encroaching orgasm.

"Since I arrived."

She bit her lip as his hand fell away from her body, but kept the dissatisfied groan from escaping while he took a few seconds to reach into his jeans pocket and pull out a foil-wrapped pack.

"Let me." She plucked it from his fingers and deftly ripped it open.

He winced as she rolled the condom down his length. Another time, she might have made more of a production of it to torment him, but her body needed to join with his, so she skipped the foreplay.

Almost as soon as she was done, he was lifting her off the floor and settling her back against the wall once more. Brandee stared out the shower door at the mirror that hung over the double vanity. She could just make out the back of Shane's head and her fingers laced in his hair. Every muscle in her body was tensed. Waiting.

"Look at me."

She resisted his demand. She needed him inside her, but she couldn't let him see what it would do to her. This wasn't just sex. Something was happening to her. In the same way she'd liked having him in her bedroom and found comfort riding beside him out in the pasture, she craved intimacy that went beyond the merely physical.

"Look at me." His rough voice shredded her willpower. "You're going to watch what you do to me."

That did it. She could no longer resist him. Her eyes locked with his. A second later he began to slide inside her, and Brandee began to shatter.

Eight

Shane wasn't sure what he'd said to make Brandee meet his gaze, but from the way her big blue-gray eyes locked on him, he was certain he'd regret it later. The ache she'd aroused needed release, but he took his time sliding into Brandee this first time. He wanted to remember every second, memorize every ragged inhalation of her breath and quiver of her body.

The first flutters of her internal muscles began before he'd settled his hips fully against hers. Her eyes widened to a nearly impossible size and she clutched his shoulders, her fingernails biting into him. As the first shudder wracked her, it was all he could do to keep from driving into her hard and fast and taking his own pleasure. Instead, he withdrew smoothly and pressed forward again. He watched in utter fascination as a massive orgasm swept over her, nearly taking him with it.

"Damn, woman." He thought he'd known lust and desire before, but something about what had just happened with Brandee told him he was diving straight off a cliff with nothing at the bottom to keep him from crashing and burning. "That was fast."

She gave him a dreamy smile as her head dropped back against the wall. Her lashes appeared too heavy to lift. "It's been a while," she said weakly. At long last her gaze found his and a mischievous glint lurked in the depths of her eyes. "And you're pretty good at this."

"You haven't seen anything."

She slid her fingers up his shoulders and into his hair, pressing the back of his head to urge his mouth toward hers. "Then let's get this party started."

"I thought we already had."

Before she could come up with another sassy retort, he claimed her mouth. Apparently the orgasm hadn't dampened her fire because Brandee kissed him back with ardent intensity.

Shane began to move inside her once more, determined to take his time and make her climax again. Had he ever been with a woman as wildly sensitive and willing to give herself wholeheartedly to pleasure as Brandee? Her whispered words of encouragement accompanied his every thrust and drove his willpower beyond its limits. But he held on until he felt the tension build in her body again. At last he let himself go in a rush of pleasure as her body bucked and she began to climax again. Sparks exploded behind Shane's eyes as they went over together.

In the aftermath, there was only the hiss of water pouring from the showerheads and ragged gasps as they strained to recover. But these were distant noises, barely discernible over the stunned, jubilant voice in Shane's head. He'd known making love to Brandee would be a singularly amazing experience, but he'd underestimated the power claiming her would have on his psyche.

"You should put me down," she said, her low, neutral tone giving nothing away. "Before something happens."

Something had already happened. Something immense and unforgettable. Powerful and scary. He was both eager and terrified to repeat the experience. But not yet. First he needed a few seconds to recover. And not just physically.

As soon as she was standing on her own, he reached to turn off the water, and the instant he took his eyes off her, she scooted out of the shower. He started to follow, but was slowed when a towel shot toward his face. The emotions that had been gathering in him, unsettling yet undeniable, retreated as he snatched the thick terry from the air.

Brandee had used his momentary distraction to slip a robe off the back of the door and wrap it around herself. Water dripped from the ends of her blond hair as she whirled to confront him, chuckling as she caught up another towel and knotted it around her head. Co-

cooned in plush white cotton, she watched him wrap the towel around his waist.

"Wow," she said with a bright laugh. "I knew that was going to be fantastic, but you exceeded my expectations."

Her delight found no matching gladness inside him. From her nonchalant cheerfulness, the experience hadn't been as transformative for her as it had been for him.

"That's me," he said, straining for a light tone. "Satisfaction guaranteed."

"I'll make sure I rate you five stars online." She yawned. "Well, it's been quite a day. And I still need to get a little work done. See you tomorrow, Delgado."

Shane had assumed there'd be a round two and now watched in stunned silence as Brandee blew him a kiss and disappeared out the bathroom door. Shane retreated to his room, shadowed by an uneasiness he couldn't shake. Chasing after her would only give her the upper hand in this wager.

Few knew his inner landscape didn't match the witty, life-of-the-party exterior people gravitated to. If he went after Brandee right now, he honestly didn't think he could pull off the cocky, charming version of himself that was his trademark.

She'd blown his mind and then walked away, leaving him hungry for more. But it wasn't so much his body that was in turmoil, but his emotions. And not because he was worried she might not be as into him as he'd thought.

"4 for 4" MINI-SURVEY

We are prepared to **REWARD** you with 2 FREE books and 2 FREE gifts for completing our MINI SURVEY!

FREE
Value Over
$20!

You'll get...

TWO FREE BOOKS & TWO FREE GIFTS

just for participating in our Mini Survey!

Dear Reader,

IT'S A FACT: if you answer 4 quick questions, we'll send you **4 FREE REWARDS!**

I'm not kidding you. As a leading publisher of women's fiction, we value your opinions… and your time. That's why we are prepared to **reward** you handsomely for completing our mini-survey. In fact, we have 4 Free Rewards for you, including 2 free books and 2 free gifts.

As you may have guessed, that's why our mini-survey is called **"4 for 4".** Answer 4 questions and get 4 Free Rewards. It's that simple!

Thank you for participating in our survey,

Pam Powers

To get your 4 FREE REWARDS:
Complete the survey below and return the insert today to receive 2 FREE BOOKS and 2 FREE GIFTS guaranteed!

"4 for 4" MINI-SURVEY

1 Is reading one of your favorite hobbies?
☐ YES ☐ NO

2 Do you prefer to read instead of watch TV?
☐ YES ☐ NO

3 Do you read newspapers and magazines?
☐ YES ☐ NO

4 Do you enjoy trying new book series with FREE BOOKS?
☐ YES ☐ NO

YES! I have completed the above Mini-Survey. Please send me my 4 FREE REWARDS (worth over $20 retail). I understand that I am under no obligation to buy anything, as explained on the back of this card.

225/326 HDL GLPL

FIRST NAME	LAST NAME

ADDRESS

APT.#	CITY

STATE/PROV.	ZIP/POSTAL CODE

HD-217-MSH17

▲ If offer card is missing write to: Reader Service, P.O. Box 1867, Buffalo, NY 14240-1867 or visit www.ReaderService.com ▲

BUSINESS REPLY MAIL
FIRST-CLASS MAIL   PERMIT NO. 717   BUFFALO, NY

POSTAGE WILL BE PAID BY ADDRESSEE

READER SERVICE
PO BOX 1867
BUFFALO NY 14240-9952

NO POSTAGE
NECESSARY
IF MAILED
IN THE
UNITED STATES

He'd intended to make love to her again and then spend the night snuggling with her.

Snuggling.

With a groan, Shane flipped open his laptop and stared at the screen, unable to comprehend anything on it. Brandee had definitely won this round. Now it was up to him to make sure that didn't happen again.

The following day, Shane agreed to meet Gabe for a drink at the TCC clubhouse bar before dinner. While he waited on his friend, he followed up on a text he'd received a few minutes earlier. The call wasn't going well.

"I thought I told you last week that I needed that changed," Shane snarled into his cell phone. "Get it done."

"Sheesh," Gabe commented as he slid into the empty seat beside Shane. "Did you wake up on the wrong side of the bed, or what?"

The question hit a little too close to home. In fact, he hadn't woken up at all. He'd never fallen asleep. After Brandee's abrupt departure the night before, he'd busied himself until two o'clock and then laid awake thinking about her and replaying what had happened between them in the shower. And afterward.

Never before had a woman bolted so soon after making love. If anyone put on their clothes and got out, it was him.

"Sorry," Shane muttered. "Things are way behind at The Bellamy and we're due to open in a couple months."

"Things are always running behind. You usually don't take it out on your contractors."

Shane wasn't about to get into why he was so cranky. Not even with his best friend. So he shrugged his shoulders, releasing a little of the tension, and sipped his scotch.

"I'm feeling stretched a bit thin at the moment," he said. "I told you that I'm helping Brandee with her ranch. It's made me lose sight of some of the details at The Bellamy and I'm annoyed at myself."

"Oh."

Just that. Nothing more.

"Oh, what?" Shane demanded, not sure he wanted to hear what his friend had to say.

"It's just this wager of yours…" Gabe looked deep into the tumbler before him as if he could find the answer to life's mysteries at the bottom.

"Yes?" Shane knew he should just let it drop, but whatever was or wasn't happening between him and Brandee was like an itch he couldn't quite reach. And if Gabe had some insight, Shane wanted to hear it.

"It's just that I know you, Shane. I've seen you around a lot of women. You like this one. I mean really like her."

His first impulse was to deny it, but instead, he said, "Your point?"

"Let's say you somehow win the bet and she falls madly in love with you. Then what?"

"I guess we keep dating."

"You guess?" Gabe shook his head. "Do you really think she's gonna want to have anything to do with the guy who made her fall in love with him so he could take away the ranch she loves?"

"I don't have to buy the ranch." In fact, after spending time on it, he didn't really want the ranch to become home to hundreds of luxury estates. "I could just tell her I changed my mind."

"Have you?"

"Maybe."

"Does anyone ever get a straight answer out of you?"

"It depends."

"And what happens if Brandee wins?"

"That's not going to happen. I might really like this woman, but that's as far as it goes. She and I are too much alike. Neither one of us is interested in a relationship. We talked about it and we agree. Sex is great. Romance is..."

He'd been about to say *tiresome*, but he had to admit that over the course of several dinners and long talks by the fireplace on the patio, he was enjoying himself a great deal.

"Romance is...?" Gabe prodded.

"Too complicated, and you know I like things casual and easy."

With a nod, Gabe finished the last of his drink. "As long as you realize what you're doing can have repercussions and you're okay with whatever happens, my job as your conscience is done."

"I absolve you of all responsibility for any missteps I make with Brandee."

Gabe didn't look relieved as he nodded.

"One last thing before we get off the topic of Brandee," Shane said, remembering his promise to her the night before. "She asked me if you'd be willing to help tomorrow with her teen group. Apparently Megan Ma-

guire from Safe Haven is bringing by some of her rescue dogs for the kids to work with."

"Sure. Let me know what time I need to be there."

Brandee surveyed the camp meeting hall for any
details left undone. It was nearly ten o'clock in the
morning and she was expecting a busload of teenagers
to arrive at any moment. Megan had brought fifteen
dogs, one for each teenager. Currently the rescues were
running around in the paddock, burning off energy.

"Thank you for helping me out today," Brandee said
to Gabe.

"My pleasure."

He and Chelsea had moved tables and organized
the kitchen, while Brandee had helped Megan with
the dogs and set up the obstacle course they would use
later in the afternoon.

The plan for the day was for Megan to talk about the
benefits of dog training for both the owner and pet and
demonstrate her preferred method of clicker training.
Then they would turn the kids loose in the paddock
with the dogs so everyone could get to know each other.

After lunch, the teenagers would be issued click-
ers and dog treats. Megan was in charge of pairing up
child with dog. Some of the kids had been through this
before, so they would be given less experienced dogs.
And the dogs that were familiar with clicker training
would be matched with newcomers.

"Have you heard from Shane?" Gabe asked. "I thought
he was going to be here today."

"He promised he would be, but he had something to check on at his hotel project."

"Well, hopefully that won't take him all day."

Brandee heard something in Gabe's tone, but before she could ask him about it, the camp bus appeared around a curve in the driveway. She pushed all thought of Shane's absence to the back of her mind. They'd completed the preliminary work without him, and there wouldn't be much to do while Megan spoke. Hopefully, Shane would arrive in time to help with lunch.

"Here we go." Megan Maguire came to stand beside Brandee. The redhead's green eyes reflected optimism. With her kind heart and patient manner, Megan was one of the most likable people Brandee had ever met. "I hope this group is as good as the last one."

"Me, too. We had such a great time."

"Of the ten dogs I brought that day, three of them were adopted almost immediately. The little bit of training they get here really helps."

"I know most of the kids enjoy it. Some act as if they are just too good for this. But it's funny, a couple of those girls that gave us such a hard time last month are back to do it again."

Brandee wasn't sure if it was because their parents were forcing them or if deep down inside they'd actually had fun. And what wasn't fun about hanging out with dogs all day?

The bus came to a halt and the door opened. The first teenager who emerged was Nikki Strait. She was one of the girls who'd been so bored and put out the prior month. She looked no better today. Neither did her best friend, Samantha, who followed her down the bus steps. Brandee sighed. Perhaps she'd been a little too optimistic about those two.

"Welcome to Hope Springs Camp," she said as soon as all the teenagers were off the bus and gathered in an ungainly clump. "On behalf of Megan Maguire of Royal Safe Haven and myself, we appreciate you giving up your Saturday to help with the dogs."

There were a couple smiles. A lot of looking around. Some jostling between the boys. All normal teenage behavior.

"We'll start our day in the camp meeting hall, where Megan will demonstrate what you'll be doing today. If you'll follow me, we can get started."

The teenagers settled into the folding chairs Chelsea had set up and more or less gave Megan their attention as she began speaking about Royal Safe Haven and the number of dogs that people abandoned each year in Royal.

"Dogs are pack animals," Megan explained. "They need a pack leader. Today it will be your job to assert yourself and take on that role. This doesn't mean you will mistreat the dogs or get angry with them. Most dogs perform better with positive reinforcement. That's why we use this clicker and these treats to get them to perform basic tasks such as recognizing their name, and commands such as *sit* and *down*. We'll also work with them on recalls and a simple but potentially life-saving maneuver I like to call 'what's this.'"

Megan set about demonstrating with her dog how effective the method was. She then switched to a nine-month-old Lab mix that had come to the shelter only the day before and was full-on crazy rambunctious.

Brandee surveyed the teens, noting which ones seemed engaged in the process and which couldn't be bothered. To her surprise Nikki was one of the former. The same could be said for Samantha.

Next, Megan brought the kids to the paddock so they could meet the dogs. Brandee turned her attention to lunch preparations. May had helped with the food. She'd fixed her famous lasagna and they would be serving it with salad, warm garlic bread and brownies for dessert. Last month they'd done chili and corn bread. As for next month…who knew if she'd even be around. With Maverick causing trouble, and Shane acting distant one minute and amorous the next, there were too many variables to predict.

A much more animated group of teenagers returned to the meeting hall. Playing with a group of dogs would do that.

Shane still hadn't arrived by the time the tables were cleared and the teenagers got down to the serious business of clicker training. Brandee shooed Gabe and Chelsea out of the kitchen with plates filled with lasagna and began the tedious job of cleaning up. She wrapped up what was left of the main meal and put the pans into the sink to soak while she nibbled at some leftover salad and scarfed down two pieces of May's delicious garlic bread.

It was almost one o'clock when Shane strolled into the meeting hall. Brandee had finished washing the

plates and the silverware. All that was left was to scrub
the pans.

"How's it going?" he asked, snagging a brownie.
Leaning his hip against the counter, he peered at her
over the dessert before taking a bite. "This is delicious."

"It's going fine," Brandee said, more than a little
perturbed that after promising to help, he hadn't. "I
didn't realize your business was going to take you all
morning. You missed lunch."

"That's okay, I grabbed something in town."

"I thought you had a meeting at The Bellamy."

"I did, then David and I needed to chat, so we
headed over to Royal Diner." He was gazing out the
pass-through toward the gathered teenagers. "I'm here
now. What can I do?"

She was tempted to tell him everything was done,
but then she remembered the lasagna pans and grinned.
"You can finish the dishes." She flung a drying towel
over his shoulder and pointed at the sink. "I always
leave the worst for last and now they're all yours."

As she went to join the others, her last glimpse of
Shane was of him rolling up his sleeves and approaching the sink as if it contained a live cobra. She doubted
the man had ever done a dish in his life and reminded
herself to double-check the pans later to make sure
they were clean to her standards.

Banishing Shane from her thoughts, Brandee circled the room to check on everyone's progress. To her
surprise, Megan had paired Nikki with the hyper Lab
mix. Nikki had seemed so disinterested the previous
month, but with the puppy, she was completely focused

and engaged. Already the teenager had the puppy sitting and lying down on command.

Brandee sidled up to Megan. "After how she was last month, what made you think to put Nikki and the Lab mix together?"

Megan grinned. "She and her mom have come by the shelter a couple times to help with the dogs and she has a real knack with them. I think last month she was bored with Mellie. This puppy is smart, but challenging. You can see how well it's going."

Next, Brandee turned her attention toward Justin Barnes. He'd isolated himself in a corner and was spending more time petting the dog than training her. It had been like this last month, too. The high school sophomore was disengaged from what was going on around him. She glanced in Gabe's direction, thinking he might be able to engage Justin, but Gabe was helping Jenny Prichard work with an adorable but very confused shih tzu/poodle mix.

Shane's voice came from right behind her. "Who's the kid over there?"

"Justin. He's the one I told you about whose dad wants him to play football rather than the guitar."

"Sounds like he and I might have a few things in common."

Brandee wasn't sure what Shane could say that might help Justin, but she'd asked for Shane to come today. It seemed wrong not to give him a chance to pitch in. "Maybe you could talk to him about it?"

"It's been a long time since I was a teenager, but I can give it a try."

"Thanks." Any animosity Brandee might have felt for his tardiness vanished. "I'll finish up the pans."

"No need. They're done."

"Already?"

"Just needed a little elbow grease." He arched an eyebrow at her. "It's not good for my ego that you look so surprised."

"I'm sure your ego is just fine." It was familiar banter between them, yet for one disconcerting moment, Brandee craved a more substantive connection. She dismissed the feeling immediately. What was she thinking? That she was interested in a *relationship* with Shane Delgado? Her stomach twisted at the thought, but the sensation wasn't unpleasant. Just troubling.

"You're right." He smirked at her. "It's great being me."

She watched him walk away and laughed at her foolishness. Even if she'd never made the bet with Shane, falling in love with him would be a disaster. They were too much alike in all the bad ways and complete opposites in the good ones. Nope, better to just keep things casual and breezy between them. Fabulous, flirty, sexy fun. That was all either of them wanted and all she could handle.

As he ambled toward Justin, Shane passed Gabe and raised his hand in greeting. Gabe acknowledged him with a broad grin and Shane wondered if he saw a touch of relief in his friend's eyes. No doubt Gabe appreciated that he was no longer the only guy.

Snagging a spare chair, Shane carried it to Justin's corner and set it down beside the kid, facing the dog.

"Hey," he said as he dropped a hand on the dog's caramel-colored head. "How's it going?"

"Fine." Justin mumbled the word and punched down on the clicker. The dog's ears lifted and he focused his full attention on the treat in Justin's hand.

"What's his name?" Shane indicated the dog.

"*Her* name is Ruby."

"Hey, Ruby." He fussed over the dog for a bit and then slouched back in his chair. "I'm Shane."

"Justin."

With niceties exchanged, the two guys settled down to stare at the dog, who looked from one to the other as if wondering where her next treat was coming from.

After a bit, Shane ventured into the silence. "What are you supposed to be doing?"

"Clicker training."

"How does that work?"

"Ruby."

The dog met Justin's glance. He clicked and gave her a treat.

"That's great."

Justin nodded.

So, obviously this whole connecting-with-kids thing wasn't easy. Shane's respect for Brandee's dedication grew. He shifted forward in the chair, propped his forearms on his thighs and mashed his palms together.

"She made me do dishes," he murmured. "Can you believe that?"

"Who did?"

"Brandee. She's always making me do stuff I don't want to."

"That sucks." Justin cast a sidelong glance his way. "Why do you do it?"

"Because she's pretty and I really like her. I'm not sure she likes me, though. Sometimes I feel like no matter what I do, it's not good enough, ya know?"

"Yeah." More silence, and then, "It's like that with my dad. He makes me play football, but I hate it."

"My dad was the same way." After all these years, Shane couldn't believe he still resented his father, but the emotion churned in him. And really, it was all about not being good enough in Landon Delgado's eyes. "He expected me to follow in his footsteps and take over the family ranch, but I hated it." And in a community dominated by ranching, it felt like treason to criticize your bread and butter.

"What did you want to do instead?" Justin was showing more interest than he had a few seconds ago.

"I dunno. Anything but ranching." Shane thought back to when he'd been Justin's age. There wasn't much he'd been interested in besides hooking up with the prettiest girls in school and hanging out with his friends. He could see where his dad might've found that frustrating.

"So what do you do now?"

"Still have the ranch. And I develop properties. Heritage Estates is mine. And right now I'm working on a luxury hotel outside town called The Bellamy."

Justin's eyes had dimmed when Shane admitted he

still had the ranch. "So you did what your father wanted you to do after all."

"The ranch has been in my family for almost a hundred years," Shane explained, deciding he better make his point awfully fast or he'd lose Justin altogether. "It wasn't as if I could walk away or sell it after my dad died. But I found a way to make it work so that I can do what I want and also respect my father's wishes."

"It isn't that easy for me."

"What do you want to do instead of playing football?" Shane asked, even though he already knew the answer."

"Play guitar and write music."

"Sounds pretty cool. How long have you been into that?"

"My dad gave me the guitar for my birthday a couple years ago."

"If your dad didn't want you to play the guitar, why did he buy you one?"

"He'd rather I play football," Justin said, his tone defensive and stubborn.

"Do you know why?"

"Because he did in high school and he got a scholarship to go to college." Justin gave a big sigh. "But I'm not that good. No college is going to want to put me on their team."

"Maybe your dad is worried about paying for your college?"

"I guess." Justin shrugged. "But I'm not really sure I want to go to college. I want to write songs and have a music career."

"You're way ahead of where I was at your age in terms of knowing what you want. That's pretty great." Shane had used money he'd inherited from his grandmother to start his real-estate development company shortly after graduating from college. When his dad found out what he'd done, he hadn't talked to him for a month. "I didn't know what I was going to do when I graduated high school, so I got a degree in business."

"College is expensive and I don't know if it would help me get what I want."

Shane wanted to argue that Justin would have something to fall back on if the music didn't work out, but he could see from the determined set of the boy's features that he would have a career in music or nothing else. Shane hoped the kid had some talent to back up his ambition.

"I'm sure this thing with your dad and football is because he's worried about your future. Maybe you could agree to try football in exchange for him agreeing to helping you with your music."

"Is that what you did with your dad?"

Not even close. "Absolutely. We came to an understanding and I figured out a way to keep ranching and at the same time pursue my interest in real estate."

"Was he proud of you?"

The question tore into Shane's gut like a chain saw. "My dad died before my business really got going, but I think he saw the potential in what I was doing and was impressed."

Shane didn't feel one bit bad about lying to the boy. Just because Shane hadn't been able to communicate with his father didn't mean Justin would have the same problem. And maybe if someone had offered him the advice he'd just given to the teenager, things with his dad might've gone better.

"I'll give it a try," Justin said.

"And if you want to talk or if you want me to have a heart-to-heart with your dad, here's my card. Call me anytime."

"Thanks." Justin slid the business card into his back pocket and seemed a little less glum. Or at least he showed more interest in the dog training.

Shane stuck around to watch him for a little while longer and then excused himself to go help a girl who seemed to be struggling with a brown-and-white mop of a dog.

Over the next thirty minutes, he worked his way around the room chatting with each kid in turn. By the time Megan called for everyone to take the dogs outside to the obstacle course, Shane had gotten everyone's story.

"How do you do that?" Brandee joined him near the back of the crowd. "Everyone you talk to was smiling by the time you walked away. Even Justin."

"How do you not realize what a great guy I am?" He grinned broadly and bumped his shoulder into hers. "I would think after living with me this past week you'd have caught the fever."

"The fever?" she repeated in a dubious tone.

"The Shane fever." He snared her gaze and gave her his best smoldering look. "Guaranteed to make your heart race, give you sweaty palms and a craving for hot, passionate kisses."

Her lips twitched. "I'm pretty sure I'm immune." But she didn't sound as confident as she once had.

"That sounds like a challenge."

"It's a statement of fact."

"It's your opinion. And if I'm good at anything, I'm good at getting people to see my point of view. And from my point of view, you're already symptomatic."

"How do you figure?"

With everyone's attention fixed on Megan, Shane was able to lean down and graze his lips across Brandee's ear. He'd noticed she was particularly sensitive there. At the same time, he'd cupped his hand over her hip and pulled her up against his side. The two-pronged attack wrenched a soft exclamation from her lips.

A second later he let her go and greeted her glare with a smirk. "Tell me your heart isn't racing."

"You aren't as charming as you think you are," she said, turning her attention to what was going on among the poles, small jumps and traffic cones set up near the meeting hall.

He let her get the last word in because he'd already annoyed her once that day and that wasn't the way to this woman's heart.

"Do you think there's something going on between Gabe and Chelsea?" Brandee asked after a couple more kids had taken their dogs through the obstacle course.

Shane followed the direction of her gaze and noticed the couple standing together on the outskirts of the crowd. "Going on how?"

"Like maybe they could be interested in each other?"

"Maybe." Shane paid better attention to the body language between the two and decided there might be an attraction, but he was pretty sure neither one had noticed it yet.

For a second Shane envied the easy camaraderie between Gabe and Chelsea. With the bet hanging over their heads, he and Brandee couldn't afford to let down their guards. And maybe that was okay. Sparring with Brandee was exciting. So was making love to her. He liked the way she challenged him, and figuring out how to best her kept him on his toes.

Besides, he wasn't in this for the long haul. This was his chance to have some fun and try to win a bet. Eventually he would move out of Brandee's house and life would return to normal. But what if it didn't? What if he wanted to keep seeing Brandee? He snuck a peek at her profile. Would she be open to continuing to see where things went? Or was this just about the wager for her?

Shane didn't like where his thoughts had taken him. He liked even less the ache in his chest. Gabe's words from several days earlier came back to haunt him.

As long as you realize what you're doing can have repercussions and you're okay with whatever happens...

It was looking more and more like he had no idea what he was doing and the repercussions were going to be a lot more complicated than he'd counted on.

Nine

To thank Chelsea, Gabe and Shane for their help at Hope Springs Camp's mini-event, Brandee treated them to dinner at the Texas Cattleman's Club. Their efforts were the reason the day had gone so smoothly and Brandee was able to relax at the end of the successful event.

As soon as they finished dinner and returned to the ranch house, she and Shane headed out to the patio to sit by the fire.

Brandee tucked her bare feet beneath her and sipped at her mug of hot, honey-laced herbal tea. "Despite your very late start," she said to Shane, keeping her tone light, "you were a huge help today. I think it was good to have both you and Gabe there. Usually we have trouble keeping the boys on task."

"A couple of them were a little rowdy while they were waiting for their turn at the obstacle course, but once they got working with the dogs it was better."

"The clicker training keeps both handler and dog engaged. Megan was very satisfied how the day went."

"She said she might even get some adoptions out of it."

"I wish Seth Houser could be one of them. He's been working with Sunny for almost three months. And making great strides." The Wheaton terrier was a great dog, but way too hyper. He'd been adopted twice and returned both times. A talented escape artist with abandonment issues, he needed to go to someone as active as he was.

"I was really amazed by how well Seth handled him." Shane puffed out a laugh. "I think Tinkerbell and Jenny were my favorite pair."

The adorable shih tzu/poodle mix with the bad underbite had been recently turned in by a woman who had to go into a nursing home. Jenny was a goth girl of fifteen who'd shuffled through the day with stooped shoulders and downcast eyes. But she'd bonded with her short-legged black-and-white dog and together they'd won the obstacle course.

"Megan has a knack for matching the right dog to the perfect handler."

They lapsed into silence for a time while the fire popped and crackled. The longer they went without speaking, the more Brandee could feel the tension building between them. The last time they'd sat together out here, she'd ended up dragging Shane into the shower.

The day after, she'd been busy with her cattle herd and hadn't gotten home until late every night. Part of her wondered if she'd been avoiding Shane. The way she'd felt as he'd slid inside her for the first time had shocked her. She'd expected to enjoy making love with Shane, but couldn't have predicted to what extent. It was like all the best sex she'd ever had rolled into one perfect act of passion.

And ever since, all she wanted to do was climb into the memory and relive it over and over. But not the aftermath when she'd bolted for the safety of her room before Shane could notice that her defenses were down. Standing naked in the bathroom, she'd been terrified that, with his appetite satisfied, he wouldn't want her to stick around. So, she'd fled.

Now, however, after a couple days to regain her confidence, she was ready to try again. Anticipation formed a ball of need below her belly button. The slow burn made her smile. She was opening her mouth to suggest they retire to his bedroom when he spoke.

"I see why you find it so rewarding."

Brandee sat in confused silence for several seconds. "What exactly?"

"Working with teenagers."

With a resigned sigh, Brandee turned down the volume on her libido. "I wish I could say it was all success and no failure, but these kids don't have nearly the sorts of issues of some I've worked with."

"You do a good job relating to them."

He hadn't done so bad himself. Watching him with Justin, Brandee had been impressed with the way he'd gotten the kid to stop looking so morose.

"I remember all too well what it was like to have troubles at home," she said.

"Your mom?" Shane asked gently.

For a second Brandee was tempted to give a short answer and turn the topic aside, but part of her wanted to share what her childhood had been like after losing her dad. "It wasn't easy living with someone who only wants you around so she can steal your money."

"I can't imagine." Shane shifted his upper body in her direction until his shoulder came into companionable contact with hers.

Brandee welcomed the connection that made her feel both safe and supported. "It didn't make me the ideal daughter."

"You fought?"

"Not exactly." Brandee let her head fall back. Her eyes closed and images of the cramped, cluttered house filled her mind. A trace of anxiety welled as memories of those five suffocating years rushed at her. "She yelled at me, while I said nothing because I'd tried arguing with her and she'd just freak out. So I learned to keep quiet and let her have her say. And then I'd rebel."

"By doing what?"

"The usual. Partying with my friends. Drinking. Drugs. For a while my grades slipped, then I realized she didn't give a damn about any of it and I was only hurting myself."

"So, what happened?"

"I cleaned up my act. Not that she noticed anything going on with me." Or cared. "But I continued to avoid the house as much as possible."

"That sounds a lot like how I spent my teen years. I made sure I was gone as much as possible. That way I wasn't around when it came time to help out on the ranch. It drove my dad crazy." Shane fixed his gaze on the hypnotic dance of the flames, but didn't seem to be seeing the fire. "He was a firm believer in hard work, a lot like your dad. He was fond of telling me I wasn't going to make anything of myself if I wasn't willing to work for it. I didn't believe him. I was pretty happy with what I had going. I had a lot of friends and decent grades. I was having a good time. And all he cared about was that I wasn't in love with ranching like he was."

Brandee didn't know how to react to the bitter edge in Shane's voice. She loved her ranch and couldn't imagine giving it up. That ranching was something Shane only did out of obligation was a disconnect between them that reinforced why she shouldn't let herself get too emotionally attached.

"What was it about the ranching you didn't like?" she asked, shifting to face him and putting a little distance between them.

"I don't honestly know. One thing for sure, I didn't see the point in working as hard as my dad did when there were more efficient ways to do things. But he wouldn't listen to anything I had to say. He expected me to follow exactly in his footsteps. I wasn't going to do that."

"What did you want to do?"

"Justin asked me that today, too. I guess I just wanted to have fun." He grinned, but the smile lacked his typical cocky self-assurance. "Still do."

She let that go without comment even as she was mentally shaking her head at him. "So, how'd you get into real-estate developing?"

"A buddy of mine in college got me into flipping houses. I liked the challenge." Satisfaction reverberated in Shane's voice. He obviously took great pride in his past accomplishments. And present ones, too. From everything she'd heard, The Bellamy was going to be quite a resort.

"I got my first job when I turned sixteen," Brandee said. "Stocking shelves at a grocery store after school and on weekends. It gave me enough money to buy a used junker with no AC and busted shocks. I didn't care. It was freedom. I used to park it around the corner from the house because I didn't want my mom knowing about it."

"What would've happened if she'd known about it?"

"She would've given it to Turtlehead or Squash Brain." Those days were blurry in her memory. "Mom always had some loser boyfriend hanging around."

"She lived with them?"

Brandee heard the concern in his voice and appreciated it more than she should. "They lived with her. She rented a crummy two-bedroom house right on the edge of a decent neighborhood because she thought it was great to be so close to people with money. I don't know what she was like when my dad met her, but by

the time I went to live with her, she wasn't what anyone would call a class act."

"What did she do?"

"She actually had a halfway-decent job. She cut
hair at one of those chain salons. I think if she had
better taste in boyfriends she might have been more
successful. But all she attracted were harmless jerks."
She thought back to one in particular. "And then Nazi
boy showed up."

"Nazi boy?"

"A skinhead with the Nazi tattoos on his arms and
all over his chest. For a while I just hung in there figuring he'd soon be gone like all the rest."

"But he wasn't?"

"No. This one had money. Not because he worked.
I think he and his white-supremacist buddies jacked
cars or ran drugs or something. He always had money
for blow and booze." She grimaced. "My mom took a
bad path with that one."

"How old were you?"

"I'd just turned seventeen."

"Did he bother you?"

"Not at first. He was more into my mom than a
dopey-looking kid with bad hair and ill-fitting clothes.
But his friends were something else. I think initially
they started to bug me out of sheer boredom. I was used
to having my ass grabbed or being shoved around by
some of the other guys my mom hooked up with. Nazi
boy's friends were different, though."

As she described her encounters, Shane's muscles
tensed. "Did they hurt you?"

She knew what he was asking. "If you're trying to be delicate and ask if I got raped, the answer is no."

Shane relaxed a little. "So what happened?"

"For a while it was okay. I was hiding behind bad hygiene and a dim-witted personality. Then one day I was taking a shower and thought I was alone in the house."

"You weren't?"

"Nazi boy had taken off with his buddies to go do something and I wasn't expecting them back. I never showered when he was home. Most days I either took clothes to school and cleaned up there or did the same thing at a friend's house."

"That's pretty extreme."

The unfinished mug of tea had gone cold in Brandee's hands, so she set it on the coffee table. "I'd seen how he could be around my mom and it made me feel way too vulnerable to be naked in the house."

"So he came home unexpectedly and caught you in the shower?"

Those days with her mom weren't something she liked talking about and part of her couldn't believe she was sharing this story with Shane. The only other person she'd told was Chelsea.

"I was coming out of the bathroom wearing nothing but a towel. The second I saw him, I jumped back into the bathroom and locked the door. He banged on the door, badgering me to open it for twenty minutes until my mom came home."

"Did you tell her what happened?"

"No. Why bother? She'd just accuse me of enticing him. Either she was scared of him or she liked the partying too much. This one wasn't going away anytime soon."

"Did he come after you again?"

"For a while I tried to stay away as much as possible, but sometimes I had to go home. When I did, I was careful to do so when my mom was home. He left me alone while she was around."

"I don't suppose you had a teacher or adult that could help you out."

"That might have been smart. But I felt like all the adults I'd reached out to had failed me. Instead, I found the biggest, meanest football player in our school and made him the most devoted boyfriend ever." She batted her eyelashes and simpered. "Oh, Cal, you're just so big and strong." Her voice dripped with honey. "Do you think you could get that terrible man who lives with my mother to stop trying to put his hands all over me?"

"Did that work?"

"Like a charm. Nazi boy was all talk and glass jaw. He knew it and I knew it. At five-ten and 170, he might have scared me, but he was no match for a six-five, 280-pound linebacker."

Shane regarded her with admiration and respect. "So your linebacker kept you safe until you finished high school?"

Brandee shifted her gaze out toward the darkness beyond the patio and debated lying to him. "I didn't actually finish high school."

"How come?"

"Because two months before graduation my mom

finally figured out that her boyfriend was coming on to me and rather than kicking him to the curb, she blamed me. That's when I ran away for good."

Shane's first instinct was to curse out her mother, but the way Brandee was braced for his reaction, he knew he had to take a gentler approach or risk her fleeing back behind her defenses.

"Wow, that sucks."

This part of her story was different than the last. As she'd spoken of her difficulties with Nazi boy, she'd sounded strong and resilient. Now, however, she was once again that abandoned child, learning that she was the biggest mistake her mother had ever made. Her loneliness was palpable and Shane simply couldn't stand to be physically separated from her. He reached for her hand and laced their fingers together, offering her this little comfort.

"What did you do?" he asked.

"I should've gone to live with my grandmother in Montana."

"Why didn't you?"

Her fingers flexed against his as she tightened her grip on him. A second later she relaxed. "Because I was angry with her for not taking me in after my dad died."

"So what did you do instead?"

"I stayed with my best friend for a couple days until I found a room and a waitressing job that paid better."

"When did you start your business?"

"I'd learned how to crochet and knit from one of my friends' moms and had been making headbands and adding lace embellishments to stuff I found at the thrift store. I bought a used sewing machine and started doing even more stuff. It was amazing how well things sold online. All I did was waitress, sew and market my stuff."

"The rest is history?"

"Not quite. Nazi boy and his friends tracked me down. Fortunately I wasn't home. But the homeowner was. They shoved her around and scared her pretty good. After that they went into my room and took everything, including the five hundred dollars I'd saved."

"What happened then?"

"The homeowner pressed charges and they all got picked up by the cops. But she kicked me out. Once again I had nowhere to go and nothing to show for all my hard work."

"Did you stay in Houston?"

"Nope. I moved to Waco and lived out of my car for two weeks."

"At seventeen?"

"Haven't you figured out I'm tougher than I look?" She gave a rueful laugh. "And I'd turned eighteen by then. In fact, I'd been out celebrating my birthday with friends when Nazi boy robbed me."

"What happened after that?"

"That's when things get boring. I found another waitressing job and another place to live. Took a second job at a tailoring shop. The owner let me use the machines after hours so I could create my designs. In four months I was making enough by selling my clothes and accessories online to quit my waitressing job. In a year I moved into a studio apartment and was bringing in nearly ten thousand a month."

Shane had a hard time believing her numbers could be real. "That's a lot for a solo operation."

"I didn't sleep, was barely eating and the only time I left my apartment was to get supplies or ship product."

"How long before it got too big for you to handle?"

"By the time I turned twenty, I had four seam-stresses working for me and I was in over my head. I was paying everyone in cash and eventually that was going to catch up to me. So I talked to a woman at the bank I really liked and Pamela hooked me up with a website designer, lawyer and an accountant. But between the designing and running things, there was still too much for me to do, so I hired Pamela to manage the business side. And then things really took off."

"And now here you are running a ranch." He smiled ruefully. "It's not an ordinary sort of career move."

"Probably not, but it's a lot better for me. While I loved designing and promoting my fashion lines, I'm not cut out to sit in an office all day looking at reports and handling the myriad of practical decisions a multimillion-dollar business requires."

"You'd rather ride around in a pasture all night, keeping an eye on your pregnant cows."

She nodded. "Exactly."

"So, you sold the business."

"A woman in California bought it and has plans to take it global." Brandee shook her head. "It's still a little surreal how much the company has grown from those first few crocheted headbands."

"I can't help but think it was a lot to give up."

"It wasn't my dream. Hope Springs Ranch is. And I still design a few pieces each year. So, I get to be creative. It's enough. And now I expect to be busier than ever with Hope Springs Camp starting to ramp up."

His gaze fastened on her softly parted lips and a moment later, he'd slid his hand beneath the weight of her long hair and pulled her toward him. After the first glancing slide of his mouth over hers, they came together in a hungry crush.

Tongues danced and breath mingled. Shane lifted her onto his lap, the better to feel her soft breasts press against him through her cotton shirt. With her fingers raking through his hair, Shane groaned her name against the silky skin of her long neck. Despite the longing clawing at him these past few days, he'd underestimated his need for her.

"I can't wait to be inside you again," he muttered, sliding his tongue into the hollow of her throat while his fingers worked her shirt buttons free. "You are like no woman I've known."

Brandee stripped off her shirt and cast it aside. "You're pretty awesome yourself, Delgado." Her fingers framed his face, holding him still while she captured his gaze. "You've made me feel things I've never known before."

Her mouth found his in a sweet, sexy kiss that stole his breath. He fanned his fingers over her back, reveling in her satiny warmth, the delicate bumps of her spine and the sexy dimples just above her perfect ass.

This time around, Shane was determined to take his time learning everything about what turned her on.

He shifted so that her back was against his chest and his erection nestled between her firm butt cheeks. This gave him full access to her breasts, stomach and thighs, while she could rock her hips and drive him to new levels of arousal. As trade-offs went, it wasn't a bad one.

Shane unfastened her bra and set it aside. As the cool night air hit her nipples, they hardened. He teased his fingertips across their sensitive surface and Brandee jerked in reaction. Her head fell back against his shoulder as a soft *yes* hissed past her teeth.

"Do that again," she murmured, her eyelids half-lowered, a lazy smile on her lips. "I love the feel of your hands on me."

"My pleasure."

He cupped her breasts and kneaded gently, discovering exactly what she liked. Each breathy moan urged his passion higher. His fingers trembled as they trailed over her soft, fragrant skin. Her flat stomach bucked beneath his palm as he slipped his fingers beneath the waistband of her leggings and grazed the edge of her panties.

"Let's get these off." His voice was whisky-rough and unsteady.

"Sure."

She helped him shimmy the clingy black cotton material over her hips and down her legs. He enjoyed sliding his hands back up over her calves and knees, thumbs trailing along the sensitive inner thigh. Catching sight of her lacy white bikini panties, Shane forgot his early determination to make her wait.

He dipped his fingertips beneath the elastic and over her sex. She spread her legs wider. Her breath was coming in jagged gasps and her body was frozen with anticipation as he delved into her welcoming warmth.

They sighed together as he circled her clit twice before gliding lower. He found a rhythm she liked, taking his cues from the way her hips rocked and the trembling increased in her thighs. She gave herself over to him. She was half-naked on his lap, thighs splayed, her head resting on his shoulder, eyes half-closed. She sighed in approval as he slid first one, then two fingers inside her.

The tension in her muscles increased as he slowly thrust in and out of her. He noted how her eyebrows came together in increased concentration, saw the slow build of heat flush her skin until all too soon, her lips parted on a wordless cry. And then her back arched. She clamped her hand over his and aided his movements as her climax washed over her in a slow, unrelenting wave. He cupped her, keeping up a firm, steady pressure, and watched the last of her release die away.

"We need to take this indoors," he murmured against her cheek, shuddering as she shifted on his lap, increasing the pressure of her backside against his erection. The sensation made him groan.

"Give me a second," she replied. "I'm pretty sure I can't walk at the moment."

Wait? Like hell.

"Let me help you with that." He lifted her into his arms and stood.

"Your room," she exclaimed before he'd taken more than two steps. "Please. I've been imagining you all alone in that big bed and thinking about all the things I'd like to do to you in it."

He liked the way her mind worked. "I've been picturing you there, as well." He slipped through the French doors and approached his bed. "We'll take turns telling each other all about it and then acting every scenario out."

"Sounds like we're going to have a busy night."

"I'm counting on it."

Tonight, he'd make sure she didn't have the strength to leave until he was good and ready to let her go.

Ten

The Royal Diner was packed at nine o'clock on Sunday morning, but Brandee had gotten there at eight and grabbed a table up front. As Chelsea slid into the red vinyl booth across from her, Brandee set aside the newspaper she'd been reading.

"Thanks for meeting me," Brandee said. "I needed to get out of the house. This thing with Shane is not going as I'd hoped."

"I told you it was a bad idea."

Brandee winced. "Let's put it down to me being in a desperate situation and not thinking straight."

"So, have you finally given in to that wild animal magnetism of his?"

"I haven't *given in* to anything," Brandee retorted. "However, we have been having fun." A lot of fun.

"You are such a fake." Chelsea laughed. "You act all cool chick about him, but I watched you yesterday. When he was talking to the kids, you were all moony. You've got it bad."

Brandee wasn't ready to admit this in the relative safety of her mind much less out loud to her best friend in a public restaurant. "It's just sex. I've been out of circulation for a long time and he's very capable."

Chelsea shook her head in disgust and picked up her menu. "Is that why you look so tired out this morning?"

"No. I actually got a good night's sleep."

That was true. After they'd worn each other out, Brandee had fallen into the deepest slumber she'd had since Maverick had sent that vile demand. Snuggling in Shane's arms, his breath soft and warm against her brow as she'd drifted off, she'd gained a new perspective on the amount of time she spent alone. Where she'd thought she was being smart to direct her energy and focus toward the ranch, what she'd actually done was maintain a frantic pace in order to avoid acknowledging how lonely she was.

"Thanks again for your help yesterday," Brandee said once they'd put in their breakfast orders and the waitress had walked away. "I couldn't have managed without you and Gabe and, once he showed up, Shane. I hope this wasn't my last mini-event."

"Anything new from Maverick?"

"No, but my resignation from the TCC and the money are due in two days. And I don't know if Shane's going to sign away his claim to Hope Springs Ranch before the deadline."

"You don't think Shane is falling in love with you?"

Brandee's heart compressed almost painfully at Chelsea's question. "I don't know. Do you think he is? Even a little?" She sounded very insecure as she asked the question.

"It's hard to tell with Shane. He hides how he feels nearly as well as you do." Chelsea eyed her friend over the rim of her coffee cup. "But given the way he looked at you during dinner last night, I'd say that he's more than a little interested."

Brandee still felt an uncomfortable pang of uncertainty. "That's something, I guess."

"Which makes the whole wager thing a bummer because it's going to get in the way of you guys being real with each other."

Thinking over the prior evening's conversation and the lovemaking that followed, Brandee wasn't completely sure she agreed. She'd felt a connection with Shane unlike anything she'd ever known before. Maybe sharing their struggles with their parents had opened a gap in both their defenses.

"I'd like to call off my wager with Shane," Brandee admitted. "What started out as a good idea has gotten really complicated."

"So do it."

"How am I supposed to explain my change of heart to Shane?"

"You could tell him that you really like him and want to start with a clean slate."

Brandee threw up her hands, her entire body lighting up with alarm. "No. I can't do that. He'll think he's won and I'll have to sell him Hope Springs."

Besides, leaving herself open to be taken advantage of—or worse, rejected—went against all the instincts that had helped her to survive since she was twelve years old. She didn't want to be that girl anymore, but she was terrified to take a leap of faith.

Chelsea blew out her breath in frustration. "This is what I'm talking about. You have to stop working the angles and just trust that he feels the same way."

"But what if he doesn't?" Already Brandee had talked herself out of canceling the wager. "What if it's just that he's done a better job of playing the game than me?"

"And what if he's really fallen for you and is afraid to show it because that means you'll win the wager? Shane loves a challenge. You two have squared off against each other almost from the day you met. Frankly, I'm a little glad this Maverick thing came along to bring you two together."

Chelsea's frustrated outburst left Brandee regarding her friend in stunned silence. She'd never considered that being blackmailed could have an upside. Yet she couldn't deny that her life was a little bit better for having gotten to spend time with Shane.

The sound of angry voices came from a table twenty feet away.

Chelsea, whose back was to the drama, leaned forward. "Who is it?"

"Looks like Adam Haskell and Dusty Walsh are at it again." The two men hated each other and tempers often raged when they occupied the same space. "I can't quite tell what it's about."

"You're nothing but an ignorant drunk." Walsh's raised voice had the effect of silencing all conversation around him. "You have no idea what you're talking about."

"Well, he's not wrong," Chelsea muttered, not bothering to glance over her shoulder.

Brandee's gaze flickered back to her best friend. "He needs to learn to mind his own damn business." She remembered how when she first bought Hope Springs Ranch, Adam had stopped by to inform her that ranching wasn't women's work.

"You're gonna get what's coming to you." Haskell's threat rang in the awkward silence that had fallen.

"You two take it outside." Amanda Battle stepped from behind the counter and waded into the confrontation. "I'll not have either of you making a ruckus in my diner."

Most people probably wouldn't have tangled with either Haskell or Walsh on a normal day, much less when they were going at each other, but Amanda was married to Sheriff Nathan Battle and no one was crazy enough to mess with her.

"He started it," Walsh grumbled, sounding more like a petulant five-year-old than a man in his sixties. It was hard to believe that someone like Dusty could be related to Gabe. "And I'm not done with my breakfast."

"Looks like you're done, Adam." Amanda glanced pointedly at the check in his hand. "Why don't you head on over to the register and let Karen get your bill settled."

And just like that it was over. Brandee and Chelsea's waitress appeared with plates of eggs, biscuits and gravy, and a waffle for them to share. She returned a second later to top off their coffee and the two women dug in.

After a while Brandee returned to their earlier conversation. "I've been thinking more and more about what Maverick brought to light."

"That it's not really fair to keep Shane from knowing that his family is the rightful owners of the land Hope Springs sits on?"

"Yes. I can't exactly afford to walk away from ten million dollars, but I can make sure that after I'm gone the land will revert back to his family."

Chelsea was silent for a long time. "This really sucks."

"Yes, it does." Brandee was starting to think that no matter what she did, her time with Shane was drawing to a close. "Whoever Maverick is, the person has a twisted, cruel personality."

"Still think it's one or all of the terrible trio?"

"I can't imagine who else." Brandee hadn't given up on her suspicions about Cecelia, Simone and Naomi. "Although it seems a little extreme even for them."

"But you've really been a burr in their blankets and I could see them siding with Shane."

"And considering what Maverick wants…"

"Money?"

"Fifty grand isn't all that much. I think Maverick asked for money more to disguise the real purpose of the blackmail, which was getting me out of the Texas Cattleman's Club." Something she could see the terrible trio plotting to do. "Regardless of what I do or don't know, the fact is that I can't afford for Shane to find out the truth."

"But if you don't win the wager, what are you going to do?"

"As much as I hate the idea, I think I'm going to do as Maverick demands."

"So, what does that mean for you and Shane?"

"I think from the beginning we were both pretty sure this thing was going to end up in a stalemate."

"So neither of you is going to admit that you've fallen for the other."

"Nope."

"And yet I'm pretty sure you've fallen for him."

"I can't let myself go there, Chels." Brandee rubbed her burning eyes and let her pent-up breath go in a ragged exhale. "There's too much at stake."

"And if the fate of your ranch didn't hinge on you admitting that you had it bad for him?"

"The problem is that it does." As much as Brandee wished she was brave enough to risk her heart, she could point to too many times when trusting in things beyond her control hadn't worked in her favor. "So, I guess that's something we'll never know."

The rain began shortly after three o'clock that afternoon. Brandee fell asleep listening to it tap on the French doors in the guest suite, a rapid counterpoint to the steady beat of Shane's heart beneath her ear. It was still coming down when she woke several hours later.

They hadn't moved during their nap and his strong arms around her roused a contentment she couldn't ignore. For as long as she could remember, she'd bubbled with energy, always in motion, often doing several things at once and adding dozens of tasks to the bottom of her to-do list as she knocked off the ones at the top.

Around Shane she stepped back from the frenetic need for activity. He had a way of keeping her in the moment. Whether it was a deep, drugging kiss or the glide of his hands over her skin, when she was with him the rest of the world and all its problems slipped away.

"Ten more minutes," he murmured, his arms around her tensing.

"I'm not going anywhere."

His breath puffed against her skin as his lips moved across her cheek and down her neck. "I can feel you starting to think about everything that needs to get done in the next twelve hours."

"I'm only thinking about the next twelve minutes." She arched her back as his tongue circled her nipple. A long sigh escaped her as he settled his mouth over her breast and sucked.

In the end it was twenty minutes before she escaped his clever hands and imaginative mouth and made her way on shaking legs to her shower. As tempted as she'd been by his invitation to stay and let him wash her back, they'd already lingered too long.

They grabbed a quick dinner of May's chili to fortify them for the long, cold night, before heading out.

With the number of cows showing signs of delivering over the next twenty-four hours, it was all hands on deck.

Icy rain pelted Shane and Brandee as they maneuvered the cows. By three o'clock in the morning, Hope Springs Ranch had seen the addition of two heifers and three steers. On a normal night, emotions would be running high at all the successful births, but a sharp wind blew rain into every gap in their rain gear, leaving the group soaked, freezing and exhausted.

Brandee cast a glance around. Although most of the newborns were up on their feet and doing well, a couple still were being tended to by their moms. That left only one cow left to go. The one Brandee was most worried about: a first-time heifer who looked like she was going to be trouble.

"We might want to take this one back to the shed," Brandee shouted above the rain, moving her horse forward to turn the heifer they'd been keeping tabs on in the direction of the ranch buildings.

Her water had broken at the start of the evening and now she'd advanced to the stage where she was contracting. They'd been watching her for the last twenty minutes and things didn't seem to be progressing.

Shane shifted his horse so that the cow was between them and they could keep her heading where they wanted. It seemed to take forever and Brandee's nerves stretched tighter with each minute that passed. As many times as she'd seen calves drop, each birth held a place of importance in her heart.

They got the heifer into the barn and directed her

into a chute. At the far end was a head gate that opened to the side and then closed after the cow stuck her head through. Once the heifer was secure, Brandee put on a long glove and moved to her back end.

"I've got to see what's going on up there," she explained to Shane, who watched her with interest.

"What can I do?"

"There's an obstetric chain, hooks and a calf puller over there." She indicated a spot on the wall where the equipment was kept. "Can you also grab the wood box propped up against the wall, as well?" Two feet square and four inches high, the box was used to brace against the heifer when she started pulling the calf out.

"Got it."

Now that they had the cow inside where it was dry and light, Brandee needed to examine the birth canal to determine the size and position of the calf. She was dreading that the calf was breeched. Most calves were born headfirst, but sometimes they were turned around, and if the legs were tucked up, it would mean she'd have to go rooting around an arm's-length distance to see if she could find a hoof and wrap the chain around it.

Brandee knew she was in trouble almost immediately. Chilled to the bone, exhausted and anticipating a hundred things that could possibly go wrong with this birth, she cursed.

"Problem?" Shane stood beside her with the equipment.

"Calf's breeched." She took the chain from Shane

and indicated the puller. "You can put that aside. We're not going to need it yet."

She hoped not at all. If she could get the calf straightened out, the cow's contractions might be able to help her. Brandee just hoped the heifer wasn't worn-out from pushing the breeched baby.

"What do you do with that?" Shane indicated the chain. It was several feet in length with circles on each end, reminiscent of a dog's choke collar.

"I need to get this around the calf's legs so I can get them straightened out. Right now its hind end is toward the birth canal and its legs are beneath it."

"Isn't this something a vet should handle?"

"Only if things get complicated." And she hoped that wouldn't happen. "I've done this before. It's just tricky and time-consuming, but doable."

"What can I do to help?"

Her heart gave a silly little flutter at his earnest question. Usually she had one of the guys helping her with this, but they were all out, tending to little miracles of their own. She could handle this.

She eyed Shane's beefy shoulders with a weary but heartfelt grin. "I'm going to let you show off your manly side."

"Meaning?" He cocked an eyebrow at her.

"You get to do all the pulling."

Her last glimpse of Shane before she focused all her attention on the cow was of his sure nod. He had his game face on. This aspect of ranching was one he'd never known, but he'd stepped up and she respected him for that.

Brandee made a loop with one end of the chain and reached in until she located the calf's legs. The snug fit and the way he was positioned meant that getting the chain over the hoof required dexterity and patience. To block out all distractions, Brandee closed her eyes and "saw" with her fingers. Before she could get the loop over the hoof, she lost the opening and the chain straightened out.

Frustration surged. The miserable night had worn her down. Feeling raw and unfocused, she pulled her arm out and re-created the loop before trying once more. It took her three attempts and ten agonizing minutes before she'd captured both hooves. She was breathing hard past the tightness in her throat as she turned to Shane.

"Okay, now it's your turn." Her voice was thick with weariness and she struggled not to let her anxiety show. "We'll do this slow. I need you to pull one side and then the other to get his hooves pointed outward. I'll let you know which to pull and when."

Working together in slow stages, they got the calf's back legs straightened so that both were heading down the birth canal. Both Brandee and Shane were sweating in the cool barn air by the time stage one was complete.

"What now?" Shane asked, stepping back to give Brandee room to move around the heifer.

"We need to get her down on her right side. It's the natural position for birthing. I want as little stress on her as possible."

Brandee slipped a rope around the cow right in front of her hip bones and tightened it while rocking her gently to get her to lie down. Once the heifer was on her side, Brandee made sure the chains were still properly positioned around the calf's cannon bones.

"Good," she said, noting that the cow was starting to contract once more. "Let's get this done."

She sat down on the ground and grabbed the first hook. When the cow contracted, Brandee pulled. Nothing happened. She set her foot against the cow for leverage and switched to the second hook. With the next contraction, she pulled again without success. This breeched baby was good and stuck.

"Let me help." Shane nudged her over and sat beside her.

After alternating back and forth between the two chains a few times, Brandee dropped her head onto her arms as frustration swallowed her whole.

"Damn it, I don't want to use the calf puller." But it was very much appearing like she'd have to.

An uncharacteristic urge to cry rose in her. She wanted to throw herself against Shane's chest and sob. Brandee gritted her teeth. She never got emotional like this.

"Come on," Shane said, bumping her shoulder with his in encouragement. "We can do this."

His focus was complete as he timed his exertions with the cow's contractions. Following his example, Brandee put her energy into willing the damned calf to move. The heifer groaned, Shane grunted and Brandee's muscles strained.

After four more contractions, they were able to get more of the legs out and Brandee felt some of the tension ease from her chest. There was still no guarantee that the calf would be alive when they were done, but at least they were making progress.

"Here," she said, shifting the wood platform and sliding it against the cow's backside between the calf's legs and the floor. Now she and Shane had a better brace for their feet. "He's starting to loosen. A few more contractions and we'll have him."

Then like a cork coming loose from a champagne bottle, the rear half of the calf was suddenly out. They scooted back to make way and then scrambled to their feet. With one final contraction and two mighty pulls from Brandee and Shane, the calf slipped free in a disgusting expulsion of amniotic fluid and blood.

Shane gave a soft whoop as he and a very relieved Brandee dragged the limp calf ten feet away from the cow.

"Is it alive?" Shane bent down and peered at the unmoving calf while Brandee peeled the sack from its face and cleared fluid from its nostrils.

"It sure is." She exuberantly roughed up its coat in a simulation of its mother's rough licking and watched it begin to draw breath into its lungs.

Shane peeled off the rubber gloves he'd donned and turned them inside out to avoid transferring the gore to his skin. "What a rush."

"It can be." Brandee released the head gate and walked out of the birthing area. "Let's get out of here so she can get up and smell her baby."

The calf still hadn't moved, but now the cow got to

her feet and managed a lumbering turn. She seemed a little disengaged from what had just happened.

"She doesn't seem too interested in her baby," Shane commented, his voice low and mellow.

"Give her a minute."

And sure enough the cow ambled over to the baby and gave him a good long sniff. This seemed to stimulate the calf and he gave a little jerk, which startled the cow for a second. Then Mama gave her baby another couple sniffs and began licking.

"What do you know." Shane gently bumped against Brandee. "Looks like we did okay."

She leaned her head on his shoulder. "We sure did."

Within an hour the calf was on its feet and Brandee wanted very badly to get off hers. Several hands had swung by to check in and thumped Shane on the back when they found out he'd participated in his first calf pulling.

"I think we can leave these two for now," Brandee said, pushing away from the railing. "I really want a shower and some breakfast."

"Both sound great."

Twenty minutes later, clean and dressed in leggings and an oversize sweater, Brandee pulled her damp hair into a topknot and padded into the kitchen, where Shane had already put on a pot of coffee and was staring into the refrigerator. He hadn't noticed her arrival and she had an unguarded few seconds to stare at him.

He'd been a huge help tonight. She wondered if he still disliked ranching as much as he had when he'd first arrived. Seeing his face light up as they'd pulled the calf free had given her such joy. She was starting to get how being partners with someone could be pretty great. Too bad there was a sinkhole the size of Hope Springs Ranch standing between them.

He must have heard her sigh because he asked, "What are you hungry for?"

He turned to look at her and she realized he was the manifestation of every longing, hope and fantasy she'd ever had. She had closed the distance and was sinking her fingers into his hair before the refrigerator door closed.

"You."

Eleven

Shane's arms locked around her as their mouths fused in a hot, frantic kiss. She was everything sweet and delicious. And sexy. He loved the way her hips moved against him as if driven by some all-consuming hunger. He sank his fingers into them and backed her against the counter.

If he'd thought she made him burn before, the soft moans that slipped out when he palmed her breast awakened a wildness he could barely contain. The big island in the kitchen had enough room for them both, but before he could lift her onto it, she shook her head.

"My room."

For an instant he froze. Over the last week, she'd made it pretty clear that her bedroom was off-limits. What had changed? He framed her face with his hands and peered into her eyes. She met his gaze with openness and trust. His heart wrenched and something broke loose inside him.

"You're the most amazing woman I've ever known," he murmured, dipping his head to capture her lips in a reverent kiss.

She melted into his body and he savored the plush give of her soft curves. Before the kiss could turn sizzling once more, Shane scooped Brandee off her feet and headed to her bedroom.

She'd left the nightstand lamps burning and he had no trouble finding his way to her bed. Setting her on her feet, he ripped off his T-shirt and tossed it aside. She managed to unfasten the button on his jeans before he pushed her hands aside and finished the job himself. Once he stood naked before her, he wasted little time stripping off her clothes.

Together they tumbled onto the mattress and rolled. Breathless, Shane found himself flat on his back with a smiling Brandee straddling him. Gloriously confident in her power, she cupped her breasts in her hands and lifted them in offering to him.

Shane's erection bobbed against her backside as he skimmed his palms up her rib cage and lightly pinched her tight nipples. He wanted what happened between them tonight to be something neither one would ever forget and tangled one hand in her hair to draw her mouth down to his.

Again they kissed with more tenderness than passion. The heat that had driven them earlier had given way to a curious intimacy. Shane kissed his way down her throat and sucked gently at the spot where her shoulder and neck came together. Her fingers bit into his shoulder as she shivered.

"You like that," he said, teasing the spot with his tongue and smiling at her shaky laugh.

"I like a lot of things that you do to me."

"Like this?" He brushed his hand over her abdomen. Her thighs parted in anticipation of his touch, but he went no lower.

"Not like that," she murmured, pushing his fingers lower. "Like this." Her back arched as he slid a finger along the folds that concealed her intimate warmth. "Almost, but not quite...there."

Her shudder drove his willpower to the brink. Sensing she'd rush him if he let her, Shane eased down her body, gliding his mouth over the swell of one breast, and then the other. Brandee's fingers sifted through his hair as she sighed in pleasure.

But when his tongue drew damp patterns on her belly, she tensed, guessing his destination. His mouth found her without the preliminaries he usually observed. This time he wasn't here to seduce, only to push her over the edge hard.

Her body bowed as he lapped at her. A moan of intense pleasure ripped from her throat. The sound pierced him and drove his own passion higher. In the last week he'd learned what she liked and leveraged every bit of knowledge to wring his name from her lips over and over.

With her body still shaking in the aftermath of her climax, she directed him to her nightstand and an unopened box of condoms. The sight of it made him smile. She'd been planning to invite him to her room. This meant that her walls were crumbling, if only a little. Was he close to winning their bet?

The thought chilled him. If she fell in love with him and he took away the ranch that meant so much to her, would she ever be able to forgive him?

He slid on the condom and kissed his way up her body. She clung to him as he settled between her thighs and brought his lips to hers for a deep, hot kiss. Her foot skimmed up the back of his leg as she met his gaze. Then she opened herself for his possession. He thrust into her, his heart expanding at the vulnerability in her expression.

She pumped her hips, taking him all the way in, and he hissed through his teeth as her muscles contracted around him. For a long second he held still, breathing raggedly. Then he began to move, sliding out of her slowly, savoring every bit of friction.

"Let's go, Delgado," she urged, her nails digging into his back. She wrapped her leg around his hip, making his penetration a little deeper, and rocked to urge him on.

"You feel amazing." At the end of another slow thrust, he lightly bit her shoulder and she moaned. "I could go like this all night." He was lying.

Already he could feel pleasure tightening in his groin. He was climbing too fast toward orgasm. He surged into her, his strokes steady and deep, then quickening as he felt her body tighten around him. She was gasping for air, hands clamped down hard on his biceps as they began to climax nearly at the same moment.

He'd discovered timing his orgasm to hers required very little attention on his part. It was as if some instinct allowed their bodies to sync.

But tonight Shane grit his teeth and held off so he could watch Brandee come. It was a perfect moment, and in a lightning flash of clarity, he realized that he'd gone and done it. He'd fallen for her. Hard. Caught off guard by the shock of it, Shane's orgasm overcame him, and as his whole body clenched with it, pleasure bursting inside him, a shift occurred in his perception.

This was no longer a woman climaxing beneath him, but his woman. He couldn't imagine his life without her in it. He wanted her in his bed. Riding beside him on a horse. Laughing, teasing, working. Yes, even working. He wanted to be with her all the time.

Stunned by what he'd just admitted to himself, Shane lay on his back and stared at the ceiling while Brandee settled against his side, her arm draped over his chest, her breath puffing against his neck. Contentment saturated bone, muscle and sinew, rendering him incapable of movement, but his brain continued to whirl.

Brandee was already asleep, her deep, regular breathing dragging him toward slumber. Yet, despite his exhaustion, something nagged at him. As perfect as their lovemaking had been, there was a final piece of unfinished business that lay between them.

Leaving Brandee slumbering, Shane eased out of bed. He needed to do this while his thoughts were clear. He suspected doubts would muddy his motivation all too soon.

The first night he'd arrived, she'd shown him the two contracts. He'd taken both copies to his lawyer to make sure there was nothing tricky buried in the language. Turned out, it had been straightforward. If he signed the paperwork, he agreed to give up all claim to the land. If she signed, she agreed to sell him the land for ten million.

Several times in the last two weeks, she'd reminded him that his contract awaited his signature in her office. He headed there now. Turning on the desk light, he found a pen and set his signature to the document with a flourish.

As he added the date, it occurred to him he was declaring that he'd fallen for her. Opening himself up to rejection like this wasn't something he did. Usually he was the one making a break for it as soon as the woman he was dating started getting ideas.

Except Brandee wasn't like the women he usually went for. She was more like him. Fiercely independent. Relentlessly self-protective. And stubborn as all get-out.

Shane reached across the desk and turned off the lamp. A second after Brandee's office plunged back into darkness, her cell phone lit up. The text message caught his eye.

Pay up tomorrow or Delgado gets your land back.

Shane stared at the message in confusion. "Your land back"? Those three words made no sense. And what was this about "pay up tomorrow"? As far as

Shane knew, Brandee owned the land outright. Could there be a lien on the property he didn't know about? Shane was still puzzling about the text as he sat down in Brandee's chair, once again turned on the lamp and pulled open her file drawer.

Her organizational skills betrayed her. A hanging file bearing his name hung in alphabetical order among files for property taxes, credit card and bank statements, as well as sketches for her upcoming clothing line. Shane pulled out his file and spread the pages across the desk.

His heart stopped when he saw the birth certificates going back several generations. He reviewed the copy of Jasper Crowley's legal document that made the Hope Springs Ranch land his daughter's dowry. After reading through the newspaper clippings and retracing his ancestry, Shane understood. Brandee intended to cheat him out of the land that should belong to his family.

Leaving everything behind, he returned to the bedroom to wake Brandee and demand answers. But when he got to the room, he stopped dead and stared at her sleeping form. He loved her. That was why he'd signed the document.

Not one thing his father had ever said to him had hurt as much as finding out he'd fallen in love with a woman who was using him.

Torn between confronting her and getting the hell away before he did something else he'd regret, Shane snatched his clothes off the floor and headed for the back door. He slid his feet into his boots, grabbed his coat with his truck keys and went out into the night.

* * *

Brandee woke to a sense of well-being and the pleasant ache of worn muscles. She lay on her side, tucked into a warm cocoon of sheets and quilts. Her bedroom was still dark. The time on her alarm clock was 5:43 a.m.

The room's emptiness struck her. There was no warm, rugged male snoring softly beside her. She didn't need to reach out her hand to know Shane's side of the bed was cool and unoccupied. After the night they'd shared, she didn't blame him for bolting before sunrise. The sex had been amazing. They'd dropped their guards after the difficult calf birthing, permitting a deeper connection than they'd yet experienced.

Part of her wanted to jump out of bed and run to find him. She longed to see the same soul-stirring emotion she'd glimpsed in his eyes last night. But would it be there? In her gut, she knew he felt something for her. No doubt he was as uncomfortable at being momentarily exposed as she'd been.

As much as she'd grown accustomed to having him around and had put aside her fierce independence to let him help, she was terrified to admit, even to herself, that she craved his companionship as much as his passionate lovemaking. But was it worth losing her ranch?

Brandee threw off the covers and went to shower. Fifteen minutes later, dressed in jeans and a loose-fitting sweater, she headed for the kitchen, hoping the lure of freshly made coffee would entice Shane.

And she'd decided to come clean about Maverick, Hope Springs Ranch and the blackmail.

Over a hearty breakfast, she would explain her fear

of losing the ranch and see if he would agree to letting her keep it for now as long as she agreed to leave it to him in her will.

While she waited for the coffee to brew, Brandee headed to her office to get the document Maverick had sent to her as well as the ones she'd found during her research. Dawn was breaking and Brandee could see her desk well enough to spy the papers strewn across it. She approached and her heart jerked painfully as she realized what she was staring at.

With her stomach twisted into knots, Brandee raced from the room and headed straight for her guest suite. The room was empty. Next she dashed to the back door. Shane's coat and boots were gone. So was his truck. Her knees were shaking so badly she had to sit down on the bench in the mudroom to catch her breath.

No wonder he'd left so abruptly during the night. He knew. Everything. She'd failed to save her ranch. She'd hurt the man she loved.

It took almost ten minutes for Brandee to recover sufficiently to return to her office and confront the damning documents. How had he known to go into her filing cabinet and look for the file she'd made on him? Had he suspected something was wrong? Or had Maverick tipped him off early?

The answer was on her phone. A text message from Maverick warning her time was almost up. But how had Shane seen it? She gathered the research materials together and returned them to the file. It was then that she noticed Shane's signature on the document revoking his claim to her land.

She'd won.

It didn't matter if Shane knew. Legally he couldn't take her ranch away from her.

But morally, he had every right to it.

Brandee picked up the document. While the disclosure she'd been about to make was no longer necessary, the solution she'd intended to propose was still a valid one.

Brandee grabbed the document and her coat and headed for her truck. As she drove to Bullseye, the clawing anxiety of her upcoming confrontation warred with her determination to fix the situation. It might be more difficult now that he'd discovered she'd been lying to him all along before she had a chance to confess, but Shane was a businessman. He'd understand the value of her compromise and weigh it against an expensive court battle.

Yet, as she stood in the chilly morning air on his front steps, her optimism took a nosedive. Shane left her waiting so long before answering his doorbell that she wondered if he was going to refuse to see her. When he opened the door, he was showered and dressed in a tailored business suit, a stony expression on his face.

She held up the document he'd signed and ignored the anxious twisting of her stomach. "We need to talk about this."

"There's nothing to talk about. You won. I signed. You get to keep the ranch."

Brandee floundered. On the way over, she hadn't dwelled on how Shane might be hurt by her actions.

She'd been thinking about how to convince him of her plan so they both got what they wanted.

"I didn't win. And there's plenty more to talk about. I know what you must think of me—"

He interrupted, "I highly doubt that."

"You think I tricked you. You'd be right. But if I lose the ranch, I lose everything." Immediately she saw this tack wasn't going to be effective. So, maybe she could give him some idea of what she was up against. "Look, I was being blackmailed, okay? Somebody named Maverick sent me the Jasper Crowley document."

"That's your story?" Shane obviously didn't believe her. "You're being blackmailed?"

"Maverick wanted fifty thousand dollars and for me to resign from the Texas Cattleman's Club." To Brandee's ears the whole thing sounded ridiculous. She couldn't imagine what would convince Shane she was telling the truth. "I should've done as I was asked, but I really thought it was..."

Telling him that she suspected Cecelia, Simone and Naomi wasn't going to make her story sound any more sympathetic. Shane liked those women. Brandee would only come off as petty and insecure if she accused them of blackmail without a shred of proof.

"Look," she continued, "I should've come clean in the beginning. Maybe we could've worked something out." She took a step closer, willing him to understand how afraid she'd been. "But when I proposed the wager, I didn't know anything about you except that for years you've been after me to sell. I didn't think I could trust you."

"Were you ever going to tell me the truth?"

The fear of opening herself up to rejection and ridicule once again clamped its ruthless fingers around her throat. "Last night…" She needed to say more, but the words wouldn't come.

"What about last night?"

"It was great," she said in a small voice, barely able to gather enough breath to make herself heard.

"You say that after I signed away my rights to *my family's* land."

Why had he? He could have torn up the agreement after finding out he owned the land, but he hadn't. He'd left it for her to find. Why would he do that?

"Not because of that," she said, reaching deep for the strength to say what was in her heart. "I say it because I think I might have fallen in love with you."

His face remained impassive, except at the corner of his eyes where the muscles twitched. "Is this the part where I say I'm not going to pursue legal action against you?"

She floundered, wondering if that was what he intended. "No, this is me talking to you without this between us." She tore the document he'd signed down the middle, lined the pieces back up and tore them again.

"Is that supposed to impress me? Do you think that document would've stood up in court?"

Brandee hung her head. "It was never supposed to get that far."

"I imagine you were pretty confident you could get away with cheating me," Shane said, the icy bite of his voice making her flinch.

"I wasn't confident at all. And I wasn't happy about it. But the ranch is everything to me. Not just financially, but also it's my father's legacy. And the camp could have done so much good." Brandee ached with all she'd lost. "But I am truly sorry about the way I handled things. I didn't do it to hurt you."

He stared at her in silence for several heartbeats before stepping back.

"You didn't."

And then the door swung shut in her face.

Twelve

Five days and four long, empty, aching nights after Shane slammed the door in Brandee's face, he slid onto the open bar stool beside Gabe at the Texas Cattleman's Club and ordered a cup of coffee.

Ignoring the bartender's surprise, he growled at his friend, "Okay, you got me here. What's so damned important?"

Gabe nodded toward a table in the corner. A familiar blonde sat by herself, hunched over an empty glass. Brandee's long hair fell loosely about her face, hiding her expression, but there was no misreading her body language. She was as blue as a girl could be.

"Yeah, so?" Shane wasn't feeling particularly charitable at the moment and didn't have time to be dragged away from The Bellamy. He had his own problems to contend with.

"You don't think there's something wrong with that picture?" Gabe nodded his head in Brandee's direction.

There was a lot of something wrong, but it wasn't Shane's problem.

"Tell me that's not why you dragged me here. Because if it is, you've just wasted an hour of my time."

Gabe's eyes widened at Shane's tone. "I think you should talk to her."

"As I explained yesterday and the day before and the day before that, I'm done talking about what happened. She screwed me over."

"In order to keep her ranch," Gabe replied, his quiet, calm voice in marked contrast to Shane's sharp tone. "She stood to lose everything. How would you have behaved if the situation was reversed and you were about to lose Bullseye?"

It wasn't a fair comparison.

"I'd say good riddance." Shane sipped his coffee and stared at the bottles arranged behind the bar. "I would've sold it years ago if I thought it wouldn't upset my mom."

"You don't mean that."

"I do."

Or he mostly did. Ranching had been in his father's blood and Shane associated Bullseye with being bullied and criticized. Every memory of his father came with an accompanying ache. He'd never be the rancher his father wanted. In some ways it had been a relief when Landon had died. There, he'd admitted it. But by admitting it, he'd lived up to his father's poor opinion of him. He was a bad son. Guilt sharpened the pain until it felt like spikes were being driven into his head.

"I've never seen you like this." Gabe leaned back in his seat as if he needed to take a better look at his friend. "You're really upset."

"You're damned right," Shane said. "She intended to cheat me out of what belongs to my family."

"But you said the land was unclaimed…"

"And what really gets me—" Shane was a boulder rolling down a steep grade "—is the way she went about it."

She'd made him fall in love with her. There. He'd admitted that, too. He was in love with Brandee Lawless, the liar and cheat.

Shane signaled the bartender. Maybe something strong was in order. "Give me a shot of Patrón Silver."

She'd ruined scotch for him. He couldn't even smell the stuff without remembering the way she'd tasted of it the first night they'd made love. Or her delight when he'd introduced her to the proper way to drink it. And his surprise when she'd poured a shot of it over him and lapped up every drop.

Shane downed the tequila shot and signaled for another.

"Are you planning on going head down on the table, too?" Gabe's tone had a mild bite.

"Maybe." But instead of drinking the second shot, Shane stared at it. "You gonna sit around and watch me do it, or are you going to make sure she gets home safe?"

"I've already taken care of Brandee." Gabe nodded his head toward the entrance, where Chelsea had appeared. "If you feel like drowning your sorrows, I'll stick around to drive you home."

Shane rotated the glass and contemplated it. He'd spent the last four nights soaking his hurt feelings in alcohol and after waking up that morning with a whopping hangover had decided he was done moping. He pushed the shot away.

"No need. I'm getting out of here."

But before he could leave, Chelsea had gotten Brandee to her feet and the two women were heading toward the door. Despite how Brandee had looked staring morosely into the bottom of her glass, she wasn't at all unsteady on her feet.

Not wanting to risk bumping into her, Shane stayed where he was and turned his back to the departing women. He couldn't risk her or anyone else noticing the way his hungry gaze followed her. She'd ditched her jeans and was wearing another of those gauzy, romantic numbers that blew his mind. This one was pale pink and made her look as if a strong wind could carry her all the way to Austin. Gut-kicked and frustrated that she still got to him, he reminded himself that she was strong, independent and could take care of herself.

"Look at you three sitting here all smug and self-important." Brandee's voice rang out and conversations hushed. "Well, congratulations, you got your way."

Gabe caught Shane's eye and gave him a quizzical look. "Any idea why she's going after Cecilia, Simone and Naomi?"

With an abrupt shake of his head, Shane returned to staring at his untouched drink, but he was far less interested in it than he was the scene playing out behind him.

"I'm not going to be around to oppose you any longer. I've resigned from the Texas Cattleman's Club. It's all yours." Brandee didn't sound intoxicated exactly. More hysterical and overwrought than anything.

"We don't know what you're—" Cecelia Morgan began, only to be interrupted.

"Where do you three get off ruining other people's lives?"

The entire room was quiet and Brandee's voice bounced off the walls. None of the women answered and Brandee rambled on.

"You must have thought it would be great fun, but blackmail is an ugly business. And it will come back to bite you in the ass."

At the mention of blackmail, Shane turned around in time to see Brandee push herself back from the table where she'd been looming over the three women. They were all staring at Brandee in openmouthed shock and fear.

Brandee punched the air with her finger. "Mark my words."

As Chelsea tugged Brandee toward the exit, the trio of women erupted in nervous laughter.

"I don't know what that was about," Simone said, her voice pitched to carry around the room. "Obviously she's finally snapped."

"It was only a matter of time," Naomi agreed, tossing her head before sipping her fruity drink.

Only Cecelia refrained from commenting. She stared after Brandee and Chelsea, her eyes narrowed and a pensive expression on her beautiful face. Moments later, however, she joined her friends in a loud replay of the clash. Around them, side conversations buzzed. News of Brandee's behavior and her wild accusations would spread through the TCC community before morning.

"She thinks those three blackmailed her?" Gabe glanced at Shane. "Did you know she was planning to resign from the TCC?"

"I don't know why she needed to. I signed her damned document giving up my right to the ranch." Yet, when Brandee had come to his house to apologize, he had refused her attempt to make amends.

"You said she tore it up."

"Well, yeah." Guilt flared. But Shane refused to accept blame for Brandee's overwrought state. "None of that had anything to do with me."

"That—" Gabe gestured at the departing women "—has everything to do with you." His features settled into grim lines. "Of all the times you should have come through and helped someone."

"What's that supposed to mean?"

Gabe looked unfazed by Shane's belligerent tone. "Everybody thinks you're a great guy. You make sure of that. You've always been the life of the party. But when it comes to helping out…" The former Texas Ranger shook his head.

Shane heard the echoes of his father's criticism in Gabe's words and bristled. "Why don't you come right out and say it? No one can count on me when it comes to things that need doing."

"Mostly you're good at getting other people to do stuff."

Shane recalled the expression on Megan Maguire's face when she'd spotted him helping out with Brandee's teen day. She'd been surprised.

And if he was honest with himself, Brandee's tactics to hold on to her land weren't all that different from his own way of doing things. He'd held back important information a time or two. And what Gabe had said about his getting other people to volunteer when there was work to be done...

Growing up, his father had accused him of being lazy and Shane had resented it, despite knowing there was a bit of truth to it. So, what was he supposed to do? Change who he was? He was thirty-five years old and far too accustomed to doing things his way.

"How is it I'm the bad guy all of a sudden?" Shane demanded. "And where do you get off making judgments about me?"

"I just want to point out that while Brandee may have manipulated you, it's not like you haven't done the same to others. She's not perfect. You're not perfect. But from watching you both, you might be perfect together."

And with that, Gabe pushed away from the bar and headed out, abandoning Shane to a head filled with recriminations and a hollow feeling in his gut.

* * *

It took until Brandee was seated in Chelsea's car before the full import of what she'd just done hit her. By the time Chelsea slid behind the wheel, Brandee had planted her face in her hands and was muttering incoherent curses.

As she felt the car begin to move forward, Brandee lifted her head and glared at her best friend. "Why didn't you stop me?"

"Are you kidding?" Chelsea smirked. "You said what half the membership has been dying to. Did you see the look on their faces?"

The brisk walk across the chilly parking lot had done much to clear Brandee's head, but she was still pretty foggy. When was the last time she'd had this much to drink? She didn't even know how many she'd had.

"All I saw was red." Brandee groaned and set her head against the cool window. "Take me to the airport. I'm going to get on a plane and fly to someplace no one has ever heard of."

Chelsea chuckled. "Are you kidding? You're going to be a hero."

"No, I'm not. No one deserves to be talked to like that. I run…" She gulped. Hope Springs Camp was an impossibility now that Shane knew he owned her ranch. "I had hoped to run a camp that gave teenagers the skills to cope with their problems in a sensible, positive way. And what do I do? I stand in the middle of the Texas Cattleman's Club and shriek at those three like a drunken fishwife." The sounds coming from the seat beside her did not improve Brandee's mood. "Stop laughing."

"I'm sorry, but they deserved it. Especially if any one or all three is Maverick."

"Do you really think it's possible they're behind the blackmail?"

"I think someone needs to look into it."

"Well, it isn't going to be me. I'm going to be sitting on a beach, sipping something fruity and strong."

"You'll get a new guy? He'll have it going on?"

Despite her calamitous exit from the TCC clubhouse, Brandee gave a snort of amusement as Chelsea twisted the Dierks Bentley song lyrics from "Somewhere on a Beach" to suit the conversation. Then, despite her dire circumstances and the fact that she'd just humiliated herself, Brandee picked up the next line and in moments the two girls were singing at the top of their lungs.

They kept it up all the way to Chelsea's house, where Brandee had agreed to spend the night. She couldn't bear to be alone in her beautiful custom-tailored ranch home that she would soon have to pack up and move out of.

Tucked into a corner of Chelsea's couch, wrapped in a blanket with a mug of hot chocolate cradled in her hands, Brandee stared at the melting mini marshmallows and turned the corner on her situation. It wasn't as if it was the first time she'd lost everything. And in the scheme of things, she was a lot better off than she'd been at eighteen, broke and living out of her car.

"I guess I get to re-create myself again," she said, noticing the first hint of determination she'd felt in days.

"I think you should fight for your ranch. Take Shane to court and make him prove the land belongs to him."

Brandee didn't think she had the strength to take Shane on in a legal battle. She was still too raw from the way he'd slammed the door in her face.

"I'll think about it."

Chelsea regarded her in concern. "It isn't like you to give up like this."

"I know, but I'm not sure."

"Brandee, you can't just walk away from a ten-million-dollar property."

"It sounds crazy when you say it, but that's what I intend to do. Legally I might be able to get a court to determine the land is mine, but I think morally it belongs to Shane's family."

"What are you going to do?"

"Sell everything and start over?" The thought pained her more than she wanted to admit, but in the last five days she'd come to terms with her loss. "I wasn't kidding about finding a beach somewhere and getting lost."

"You can't seriously be thinking of leaving Royal?"

The pang in Chelsea's voice made Brandee wince. "I don't know that I want to stay here after everything that's happened." Just the thought of running into Shane and seeing his coldness toward her made her blood freeze. "Look, it's not like I have to do anything today. It's going to take me a while to sell my herd and settle things on the ranch. With The Bellamy still under construction and taking up all his energy, Shane isn't going to have time to start developing the ranch right away."

"And maybe you and Shane can work out an arrangement that will benefit you both."

"Did you see the way he acted as if I didn't exist?" Brandee shook her head, fighting back the misery that was her constant companion these days. "No, he hates me for what I tried to do to him and there's no going back from that."

"Now, aren't you glad we warned you off of Brandee Lawless?"

"Did you see how she spoke to us?"

"I think she had too much to drink. And happy hour's barely started."

"I've said from the beginning that she has no class."

"She must've had a reason for going after you," Shane said.

He recalled what had happened to Wesley Jackson, and thought there'd been some buzz around the clubhouse that Cecelia had been behind it. An anonymous hacker had exposed Wes as a deadbeat dad on social media and it had blown a major business deal for him. What had happened to Brandee was in the same vein.

"She's been out to get us from the moment we joined the Texas Cattleman's Club."

"That's not true," Shane said, a hint of warning in his tone. "She just hasn't bought into what you want to do with the place. A lot of people haven't."

"But she's been actively working to drum up resistance," Naomi said.

"That doesn't make her your enemy." Shane shook his head. "Not everyone wants the clubhouse to undergo any more changes, especially not the kind you're interested in making."

"Well, it doesn't matter anymore. She resigned her membership."

"And with her gone, the others will come around," Cecelia said. "You'll see."

"Sounds like everything is going your way." Shane set his hands on their table the way Brandee had and leaned forward to eye each woman in turn. "If I find out any of you three were behind what happened to Brandee, you'll have to answer to me."

He loomed menacingly for several heartbeats, taking in each startled expression in turn. Instinctively, they'd leaned back in their chairs as if gaining even a small amount of distance would keep them safe. At long last, satisfied they'd received his message, he pushed upright, jostling the table just enough to set their cutlery tingling and their drinks sloshing.

"Ladies." With a nod, he headed for the exit.

Icy gusts blew across the parking lot as Shane emerged from the clubhouse. He faced the north wind and lifted his hat, not realizing how angry he'd been until he dashed sweat from his brow. Damn Brandee for making him rush to defend her. He should've left well enough alone.

The cold reduced his body temperature to normal

as he headed toward his truck. A row back and a few spaces over, he caught sight of her vehicle.

"Great."

Now he'd have to make sure she wasn't driving in her condition. But the truck was empty. Brandee was long gone. Shane headed to his own truck.

As he drove the familiar roads on his way to The Bellamy, he tried to put Brandee out of his thoughts, but couldn't shake the image of her going after Cecelia, Simone and Naomi. The outburst had shocked more than a few people.

Brandee's public face was vastly different from the one she showed in private. Not once in all the years that he'd pursued her to sell the ranch had she ever cracked and lost her temper with him. Because of her cool, composed manner, he'd worked extra hard to get beneath her skin. From getting to know her these last two weeks, he recognized that she put a lot of energy into maintaining a professional image. It was why she was so well respected at the male-dominated Texas Cattleman's Club.

Today, she'd blown that. Her words came back to him. Why had she quit the TCC? Did she really think he had any intention of taking her ranch? Then he thought about how she'd torn up the document he'd signed, relinquishing his claim. The damned woman was so stubborn she probably figured she'd turn the place over to him regardless of what he wanted.

And if she did? What would she do? Where would she go? The ranch was everything to her. With her capital tied up in her land and her cows, she probably figured she'd have to downsize her herd in order to start over.

After checking to make sure everything was on track at The Bellamy, he headed home and was surprised to see his mother's car as well as a catering van in the driveway. Shane parked his truck, drawing a blank. He was pretty sure he'd remember if there was a party scheduled.

When it hit him, he cursed, belatedly remembering he'd promised his mother to help her make catering decisions this afternoon for the party being held in four weeks to celebrate Bullseye's hundred-year anniversary. He'd neglected to add the appointment to his calendar any of the four times she'd reminded him of the event.

He rushed into the house and found everything set up in the dining room. "Hello, Mother." He circled the table to kiss the cheek she offered him.

"You're late," she scolded, more annoyed than she sounded.

The way she looked, he was going to need a drink. "I'm sorry."

"Well, at least you're here now, so we can begin."

Until that second, Shane had been hoping that his mother had already sampled everything and made her decisions. Now he regarded the food spread over every available inch of table and groaned. The appetizers ran the gamut from individual ribs glazed in sweet-smelling barbecue sauce to ornate pastries begging to be tasted. Three champagne flutes sat before Elyse.

She gestured toward the dining chair nearest her with a fourth glass.

"Vincent, please pour my son some champagne so he can give his opinion on the two I'm deciding between."

"I'm sure whatever you decide is fine," Shane said, edging backward. He was in no mood to sit through an elaborate tasting.

"You will sit down and you will help me decide what we are going to serve at your party."

If her tone hadn't been so severe, he might have protested that the party hadn't been his idea and he couldn't care less what they served. But since he'd already alienated Gabe today and ruined any hope of future happiness with the woman he loved several days earlier, Shane decided he needed at least one person in his corner.

It took a half an hour to taste everything and another fifteen minutes for them to narrow it down to ten items. Elyse generously included several selections Shane preferred that she'd described as too basic. He wondered if she gave him his way in appreciation of his help tonight or if it was a ploy to make him more pliable the next time she asked for his assistance.

And then he wondered why he was questioning his mother's motives. Was this what playing games had turned him into? Had he become suspicious of his own mother?

And what about Brandee? Was she solely to blame for the way she'd tried to trick him? If he'd been more like Gabe, honest and aboveboard, might she have come to him and negotiated a settlement that would have benefited both of them? Instead, because he liked to play games, she'd played one on him.

"I'm sorry I forgot about today," he told his mother as Vincent packed up his edibles and returned the kitchen to its usual pristine state.

She sipped champagne and sighed. "I should be used to it by now."

Shane winced. With Gabe's lecture foremost in his thoughts, he asked, "Am I really that bad when it comes to getting out of doing things?"

"You're my son. And I love you." She reached out and patted his hand. "But when it comes to doing something you'd rather avoid, you're not very reliable."

It hurt more than he imagined it would to hear his mother say those words. Realizing he wasn't his mother's golden child humbled Shane. "Dad yelled at me about that all the time, but you never said a word."

"Your father was very hard on you and it certainly decreased your willingness to help around the ranch. You didn't need to feel ganged up on."

From where he was sitting, he could see the informal family portrait taken when he'd been seventeen. His father stood with his arm around his beaming wife and looked happy, while Shane's expression was slightly resentful. He'd always hated it because he was supposed to be on a hunting trip with friends the weekend the photo shoot had been scheduled. The photo seemed to sum up how he'd felt since he was ten.

Mother and son chatted for over an hour after the caterer departed about Elyse's upcoming trip to Boston for her brother Gavin's surprise sixty-fifth birthday party. She and Gavin's wife, Jennifer, were planning a tropical-themed bash because Gavin was also retiring at the end of the month and he and Jennifer were going to Belize to look at vacation properties.

"I need to get going," Elyse said, glancing at her watch. "I promised Jennifer I would call her to firm up the last few details for Gavin's party." She got to her feet and deposited a kiss on Shane's cheek. "Thank you for helping me today."

"It was my pleasure." And in fact, once he got over his initial reluctance, he'd enjoyed spending time with his mom, doing something she took great pride in. "Your party-planning skills are second to none and the centennial is going to be fantastic. Let me know what else I can do to help you."

His mother didn't try to hide her surprise. "You mean that?"

"I do. Send me a list. I'll get it done."

"Thank you," she said, kissing him on the cheek.

After his mom left, Shane remembered something else he'd been putting off. His keys jingled as he trotted down the steps to the driveway. He needed to pick up his stuff from Brandee's. He'd been in such a hurry to leave that he hadn't taken anything with him.

He didn't expect to see her truck in the driveway and it wasn't. It was nearly seven o'clock. The sun was below the horizon and a soft glow from the living room lights filled the front windows. Shane got out of his truck and headed for the front door, remembering the first time he'd stepped onto her porch two weeks ago. So much had happened. So much had gone wrong.

First he tried the doorbell, but when that went un-answered, he tried knocking. Was she avoiding him? Or had she come home, consumed more alcohol and passed out? Shane decided he needed to see for him-self that she was okay and used the key she'd given him to unlock the door.

As he stepped across her threshold, he half expected her to come tearing toward him, shrieking at him to get out. Of course, that wasn't her style. Or he hadn't thought it was until he'd witnessed her going after Cecelia, Simone and Naomi today.

He needn't have worried. The house had an unoc-cupied feel to it.

A quick look around confirmed Brandee hadn't come home. Shane headed to the guest suite and was surprised to find none of his things had been touched. Moving quickly, he packed up his toiletries and clothes. He kept his gaze away from the luxurious shower and the big, comfortable bed. Already a lump had formed in his throat that had no business being there. He swal-lowed hard and cursed.

What the hell had he expected? That they would live happily-ever-after? Even before he found out she'd been keeping the truth from him about the ranch, that ending hadn't been in the cards. All along Brandee had said she didn't need anyone's help. She'd never wanted a partner or a long-term lover. They might have enjoyed each other's company for a while, but in the end both of them were too independent and afraid of intimacy for it to have worked.

Eager to be gone, Shane strode toward the front door, but as he reached it, a familiar ringtone began playing from the direction of the kitchen. He stopped walking and, with a resigned sigh, turned toward the sound. Brandee had left her smartphone on the large concrete island.

Though he knew he should just leave well enough alone, Shane headed to check out who might be calling. Brandee always made a point of being available to her ranch hands and with her not being home, they would have no way of knowing how to get in contact with her.

Shane leaned over and peered at the screen. Sure enough, it was her ranch foreman. Now Shane had two choices. He could get ahold of Chelsea and see if Brandee was staying there, or he could find out what was up and then call Chelsea.

"Hey, Jimmy," Shane said, deciding to answer the call. "Brandee isn't around at the moment. She left her phone behind. Is there something you need?"

"Is she planning on coming back soon?"

Shane recalled how she'd looked earlier. "I doubt it. She went into town and I think she might be staying the night at Chelsea's. Is there something wrong?"

"Not wrong, but we've got a half-dozen cows showing signs of calving and she said if we needed her to help out tonight to call. But it's okay, we'll make do."

As Jimmy was speaking, Shane's gaze fell on something he hadn't noticed before. A large poster was tacked on the wall near the door to the mudroom. It held pictures of all the teenagers and their dogs surrounding a big, glittery thank-you in the middle. It was a gaudy, glorious mess and Shane knew that Brandee loved it.

He closed his eyes to block out the sight. Brandee didn't have to give her time or energy to a bunch of troubled kids, but she did it because even small events like the one with the rescue dogs had the power to change lives. He'd seen firsthand how her program had impacted each of the teens in some way, and with her camp she was poised to do so much more.

"Why don't I stop down and give you a hand." The last thing he wanted was to spend an endless, freezing night outside, but he knew it was the right thing to do.

"That would be a big help." Jimmy sounded relieved. "But are you sure? Between the cold and the number of cows ready to go, it's going to be a long, miserable night."

"I'm sure. See you in ten."

The way Shane was feeling at the moment, he was going to be miserable regardless. And to his surprise, as he headed back to the guest suite to change into work clothes, his mood felt significantly lighter. Maybe there was something to this helping-others thing after all.

Thirteen

Brandee came awake with a jolt and groped for her cell phone. Jimmy was supposed to check in with her last night and let her know if he needed her help with the calving. Had she slept through his call? That had never happened before.

Yet here she was, six short days after her reckoning with Shane, and already she was disengaging from her ranch. Had she really given up on her dream so easily? She couldn't imagine her father being very proud of her for doing so. And yet what choice did she have? All her capital was tied up in the land and her livestock. With the land returned to Shane, she didn't have a place for her cows and calves. It only made sense to sell them.

When she didn't find her phone on the nightstand, she realized why. This wasn't her room. She'd spent the night at Chelsea's after making a scene at the Texas Cattleman's Club. Brandee buried her face in the pillow and groaned. She hadn't been anywhere near drunk, but her blood had been up and she'd consumed one drink too many.

Thank goodness she'd never have to set foot in the clubhouse again. Of course, that didn't mean she wouldn't be running into members elsewhere. Maybe she could hide out for a month or so while she settled her business with the ranch stock and figured out what to do next.

Should she move away from Royal? The thought triggered gut-wrenching loneliness and crippling anxiety. She couldn't leave behind so many wonderful friends. Two weeks ago, she might have considered herself self-sufficient, but after living with Shane she realized she was way needier than she'd let herself believe.

After sliding out of bed and feeling around the floor, Brandee broke down and turned on the bedside light. Her cell phone wasn't beneath the bed or lost among the sheets. Feeling a stir of panic, she considered all the places she might've left it.

A quick glance at the clock told her it was six o'clock in the morning. Too early for Chelsea to be awake, and Brandee would not borrow her friend's computer to check on her phone's location without permission. She could, however, use Chelsea's landline to call her foreman.

He answered after the third ring. "Hey, boss."

"I can't find my phone. I'm sorry I didn't check in sooner. Is everything okay?"

"It was a pretty crazy night, but me and the boys handled it."

"That's great to hear. I'm sorry I wasn't there to help you out."

"It's okay. Shane said you were staying the night at Chelsea's."

A jolt of adrenaline shot through her at Jimmy's words. "How is it you spoke with Shane?" Annoyance flared. Was he already taking over her ranch?

"He answered your phone when I called."

"Did he say how he'd gotten my phone?" Had she left it in the parking lot of the Texas Cattleman's Club?

"He said you left it at your house." Jimmy's voice held concern. "You okay?"

For a long moment Brandee was so incensed she couldn't speak. What the hell was Shane doing in her house? "I'm fine. I need to get my truck and then I'll be by. Maybe an hour and a half, two hours tops." Cooling her heels for an hour until it was reasonable to wake Chelsea was not going to improve her temper.

"No rush. As I said, we have everything under control."

To keep herself busy, Brandee made coffee and foraged in Chelsea's pantry for breakfast. She wasn't accustomed to sitting still, and this brought home just how hard it was going to be to give up her ranch.

As seven o'clock rolled around, she brought a cup of coffee to Chelsea's bedside and gently woke her friend.

"What time is it?"

"Seven." Brandee winced at Chelsea's groan. "I made coffee," she said in her most beguiling voice.

"How long have you been up?"

"An hour." She bounced a little on the springy mattress.

"And how much coffee have you had?"

She extended the coffee so the aroma could rouse Chelsea. "This is the last cup."

"You drank an entire pot of coffee?"

"I didn't have anything else to do. I left my phone at home and didn't want to use your computer. I think the boys had a rough night and need me back at the ranch."

Chelsea lifted herself into a sitting position and reached for the coffee. "Give me ten minutes to wake up and I'll take you to your truck."

"Thank you." She didn't explain about how Jimmy had spoken with Shane or the anxiety that overwhelmed her at the thought of him giving orders to her hands.

An hour later, Brandee had picked up her truck, driven home, changed clothes and was on the way to the ranch buildings. A familiar vehicle was parked beside the barn where they kept the cows and calves who needed special attention. Brandee pulled up alongside and shut off her engine. It ticked, cooling as she stared toward the barn.

What was Shane doing here?

Brandee slid from the truck and entered the barn. She found Shane standing in front of the large enclosure that housed the breeched calf they'd brought into the world. He stood with his arms on the top rail of the pen, his chin resting on his hands.

"Hey," she said softly, stepping up beside him and matching his posture. "What are you doing here?"

"Jimmy said these two are ready to head to the pasture today."

"So you came to say goodbye?" The question didn't come out light and unconcerned the way she'd intended. Anxiety and melancholy weighed down her voice.

"Something like that."

Since Brandee didn't know what to make of his mood, she held her tongue and waited him out. She had nothing new to say and reprising her apology wouldn't win her any points. The silence stretched. She could ask him again why he'd come out to the ranch or she could demand to know why he'd entered her house without asking.

He probably figured he was entitled to come and go anytime he wanted since the land beneath the house belonged to him. Frustration built up a head of steam and she took a deep breath, preparing to unleash it. But before she could utter a word, Shane pushed away from the fence.

"I'd better go." He looked into her eyes, tugged at the brim of his hat in a mock salute and turned away.

Deflated, Brandee watched him go. She couldn't shake the feeling that she'd missed an opportunity to say or do something that would span the gap between them. Which was ridiculous. Shane hated her. She'd tricked him into giving up all claim to his family's land and he would never forgive her.

Her throat closed around a lump and suddenly she couldn't catch her breath. Tears collected and she wiped at the corners of her eyes before the moisture could spill down her cheeks. All at once she was twelve again and hearing the news that her dad was dead. Faced with an equally uncertain future, she'd gotten on her horse and rode off.

She'd ridden all day, tracing the familiar paths that she'd traveled beside her dad. At first she'd been scared. Where would she go? Who would take her in? Her mother's abandonment had hit her for the first time and she'd cried out all her loneliness and loss until she could barely breathe through the hysterical, hiccupping sobs. Once those had passed, she'd been an empty vessel, scrubbed clean and ready to be filled with determination and stubbornness.

She felt a little like that now. Empty. Ready to be filled with something.

Leaving the cow and calf, Brandee headed for the horse barn and greeted her ranch hands. They looked weary, but smiled when they saw her. Apparently the cows had kept them busy, but the night had passed without serious incident. Next she headed to the ranch office to look for Jimmy. Her foreman was staring blankly at the computer, a full mug of coffee untouched beside the keyboard.

"You should head off," she told him, sitting in the

only other chair. "I can handle entering the information."

"Thanks. I'm more beat than I thought."

"I'm sorry I wasn't here," she said again, pricked by guilt.

"It's okay. We had Shane's help and everything worked out fine."

"Shane was here all night?" Brandee's heart jumped.

"He came right after answering your phone. About seven or so."

Shane had been helping out at her ranch for over twelve hours? Why hadn't he said anything just now? Maybe he'd been waiting for her to thank him. If she'd known, she would have. Damn. No wonder he'd left so abruptly. She'd screwed up with him again.

But this she could fix. She just needed to come up with a great way to show her appreciation.

Shane wasn't exactly regretting that he'd promised his mother he'd help with Bullseye's centennial party, but he was starting to dread her texts. This last one had summoned him back to the ranch on some vague request for his opinion.

He parked his truck next to her Lexus and took the porch steps in one bound. Entering the house, he spied her in the living room and began, "Mother, couldn't this have waited..." The rest of what he'd been about to say vanished from his mind as he noticed his mother wasn't alone.

"Oh good." Elyse Delgado got to her feet. "You're home."

Shane's gaze locked on Brandee and his heart stopped as if jabbed by an icicle. "What is she doing here?"

"Shane, that's rude. I raised you better than that." Elyse set her hands on her hips and glared at her son. "She came to see me about this disturbing business about her ranch belonging to our family."

"Let me get this straight," Shane began, leveling his gaze on Brandee. "You called my mother to intervene on your behalf?"

"She did no such thing."

"It was Gabe's idea," Brandee said, a touch defensive. "He said you'd listen to her."

It was all too much. First Gabe, now his mother. Shane crossed to the bar and poured himself a shot of scotch. As soon as he lifted it to his lips, he recognized his mistake and set it back down.

"I don't know what you want," he said, dropping two ice cubes into a fresh glass and adding a splash of vodka.

"I brought this as a thank-you for helping out at the ranch the other night." While he'd had his back turned, she'd approached and set a bottle on the bar beside him.

"I don't want your thanks." Mouth watering, he eyed the rare vintage. "Besides, you've ruined scotch for me." He lifted his glass of vodka and took a sip. It took all his willpower not to wince at the taste.

Her lips curved enticingly. "It's a thirty-five-year-old Glengoyne. Only five hundred were released for sale."

"You can't bribe me to like you."

At his aggressive tone, all the light went out of her eyes. Once again she became the pale version of herself, the disheartened woman hunched over an empty glass in the TCC clubhouse.

"Shane Robert Delgado, you come with me this instant." Elyse didn't bother glancing over her shoulder to see if her son followed her toward the French doors leading out to the pool deck. She barely waited until the door had shut behind him before speaking. "How dare you speak to Brandee like that. She's in love with you."

"She tried to cheat us out of our family's land." He tried for righteous anger but couldn't summon the energy. The accusation had lost its impact.

"I don't care. We have more than enough wealth and Bullseye is one of the largest ranches around Royal. Besides, that land was unclaimed for over a hundred years and she paid for it fair and square. If anyone cheated us, it was the person who claimed the land without doing due diligence on the property's heirs."

"So, what do you want me to do? Be friends with her again?"

"I'd like for you to give up feeling sorry for yourself and tell that girl how much she means to you."

"What makes you think she means anything to me?"

"From what I hear, you've been an ornery, unlikable jerk this last week and I think it's because you love that girl and she hurt you."

Shane stood with his hands on his hips, glaring at

his mother, while in his chest a storm raged. He did love Brandee, but the emotion he felt wasn't wondrous and happy. It was raw and painful and terrifying.

"Now," his mother continued, her tone calm and practical. "I'm going to go home and you are going to tell that girl that you love her. After which the two of you are going to sit down and figure out a way to get past this whole 'her ranch, our land' thing. Because if you can't, she told me she's going to sell everything and leave Royal. You'll never see her again and I don't think that's what you want."

Shane stared out at the vista behind the ranch house long after the French door closed behind his mother.

When he reentered the house, Brandee was still standing by the bar where he'd left her. "You're still here."

"I came with your mother and she refused to give me a ride back to her house, where my truck is parked." She took a step in his direction and stopped. After surveying his expression for several seconds, her gaze fell to his feet. "Look, I'm sorry about what I did. Whatever you want me to do about the land, I will."

"I don't give a damn about the land and I'm certainly not going to kick you off and take away everything you worked so hard to build." He sucked in a shaky breath.

This was his chance to push aside bitterness and be happy. He'd lost his father before making peace with him and was haunted by that. Losing Brandee would make his life hell.

"What I want more than anything is…" He dug the heels of both hands into his eyes. Deep inside he recognized that everything would be better if he just spoke what was in his heart. Shane let his hands fall to his sides and regarded her with naked longing. "You."

Her head came up. Tears shone in her eyes as she scanned his expression. "Are you sure?" she whispered, covering her mouth and staring at him with a look of heartbreaking hope.

"I am." Shane crossed the distance between them and put his arms around her. For the first time in a week, everything was perfect in his world. "I love you and I can't bear to spend another second apart."

His lips claimed hers, drinking in her half sob and turning it into a happy sigh.

When he finally let her come up for air, she framed his face with her fingers and gazed into his eyes. "Then you're not mad at me anymore?"

"For what? Trying to save your ranch and your dreams?" He shook his head. "I don't think I was ever really angry with you for that. I fell in love with you and when I found the documents I thought you'd been playing me the whole time."

"I should have told you about the blackmail after we made love that first time. I knew then that I was falling for you, but I didn't know how to trust my feelings and then there was that stupid bet." She shook her head.

"You weren't the only one struggling. I lost interest in your land after the tornado tore through Royal. I only agreed to the wager to spend time with you. All along I'd planned to lose."

She stared at him, an incredulous expression spreading across her features. "Then why did you work so hard to win?"

"Are you kidding?" He chuckled. "The bet was for you to fall for me. That was the real prize."

"I love you." Brandee set her cheek against his chest and hugged him tight. "I can't believe I'm saying this, but I'm really glad Maverick blackmailed me. If it hadn't happened, I never would've invited you to move in."

Shane growled. "I'll buy Maverick a drink and then knock his lights out."

"We don't know who he or she is."

"I asked Gabe to investigate. He'll figure out who Maverick is." Shane scooped Brandee off her feet and headed for the master suite. "In the meantime, I'd like to see how you look in my bed."

Brandee laughed and wrapped her arms around his neck. "I'm sure not much different than I looked in mine."

There she was wrong. As he stripped off her lacy top and snug jeans, the shadows he'd often glimpsed in her eyes were gone. All he could see was the clear light of love shining for him. There was no more need for either of them to hide. This was the first step toward a new partnership. In love and in life.

With her glorious blond hair fanned across his pillow and her blue-gray eyes devouring his body while he peeled off his clothes, Shane decided she was the most incredible woman he'd ever known.

He set his knee on the bed and leaned forward to frame her cheek with his fingers. His thumb drifted over her full lower lip. "You're looking particularly gorgeous today."

She placed her hand over his and turned to drop a kiss in his palm. With her free hand, she reached up to draw him down to her. "You're not looking so bad yourself, Delgado."

And when their lips met, both were smiling.

* * * * *

Don't miss a single installment of the
TEXAS CATTLEMAN'S CLUB: BLACKMAIL.
No secret—or heart—is safe in Royal, Texas...

January 2017: THE TYCOON'S SECRET CHILD
by USA TODAY *bestselling author Maureen Child*

February 2017: TWO-WEEK TEXAS SEDUCTION
by Cat Schield

March 2017: REUNITED WITH THE RANCHER
by USA TODAY *bestselling author Sara Orwig*

April 2017: EXPECTING THE BILLIONAIRE'S BABY
by Andrea Laurence

May 2017: TRIPLETS FOR THE TEXAN
by USA TODAY *bestselling author Janice Maynard*

June 2017: A TEXAS-SIZED SECRET
by USA TODAY *bestselling author Maureen Child*

July 2017: LONE STAR BABY SCANDAL
by Golden Heart® Award winner Lauren Canan

*August 2017: TEMPTED BY THE WRONG TWIN
by* USA TODAY *bestselling author Rachel Bailey*

*September 2017: TAKING HOME THE TYCOON
by* USA TODAY *bestselling author Catherine Mann*

*October 2017: BILLIONAIRE'S BABY BIND
by* USA TODAY *bestselling author
Katherine Garbera*

*November 2017: THE TEXAN TAKES A WIFE
by* USA TODAY *bestselling author Charlene Sands*

*December 2017: BEST MAN UNDER THE
MISTLETOE by* USA TODAY *bestselling author
Kathie DeNosky*

* * *

*If you're on Twitter, tell us what you think of
Harlequin Desire! #harlequindesire*

If you like sexy and steamy stories with strong heroines and irresistible heroes, you'll love FORGED IN DESIRE by New York Times bestselling author Brenda Jackson—featuring Margo Connelly and Lamar "Striker" Jennings, the reformed bad boy who'll do anything to protect her, even if it means lowering the defenses around his own heart...

Turn the page for a sneak peek at FORGED IN DESIRE!

PROLOGUE

"FINALLY, WE GET to go home."

Margo Connelly was certain the man's words echoed the sentiment they all felt. The last thing she'd expected when reporting for jury duty was to be sequestered during the entire trial...especially with twelve strangers, more than a few of whom had taken the art of bitching to a whole new level.

She was convinced this had been the longest, if not the most miserable, six weeks of her life, as well as a lousy way to start off the new year. They hadn't been allowed to have any inbound or outbound calls, read the newspapers, check any emails, watch television or listen to the radio. The only good thing was, with the vote just taken, a unanimous decision had been reached and justice would be served. The federal case against Murphy Erickson would finally be over and they would be allowed to go home.

"It's time to let the bailiff know we've reached a decision," Nancy Snyder spoke up, interrupting Margo's thoughts. "I have a man waiting at home, who I haven't seen in six weeks, and I can't wait to get to him."

Lucky you, Margo thought, leaning back in her chair.

She and Scott Dylan had split over a year ago, and the parting hadn't been pretty.

Fortunately, as a wedding-dress designer, she could work from anywhere and had decided to move back home to Charlottesville. She could be near her uncle Frazier, her father's brother and the man who'd become her guardian when her parents had died in a house fire when she was ten. He was her only living relative and, although they often butted heads, she had missed him while living in New York.

A knock on the door got everyone's attention. The bailiff had arrived. Hopefully, in a few hours it would all be over and the judge would release them. She couldn't wait to get back to running her business. Six weeks had been a long time away. Lucky for her she had finished her last order in time for the bride's Christmas wedding. But she couldn't help wondering how many new orders she might have missed while on jury duty.

The bailiff entered and said, "The judge has called the court back in session for the reading of the verdict. We're ready to escort you there."

Like everyone else in the room, Margo stood. She was ready for the verdict to be read. It was only after this that she could get her life back.

"FOREMAN, HAS THE jury reached a verdict?" the judge asked.

"Yes, we have, Your Honor."

The courtroom was quiet as the verdict was read. "We, the jury, find Murphy Erickson guilty of murder."

Suddenly Erickson bowled over and laughed. It

made the hairs on the necks of everyone in attendance
stand up. The outburst prompted the judge to hit his
gavel several times. "Order in the courtroom. Coun-
selor, quiet the defendant or he will be found in contempt of court."

"I don't give a damn about any contempt," Erickson snarled loudly. "You!" he said, pointing a finger
at the judge. "Along with everyone else in this courtroom, you have just signed your own death warrant.
As long as I remain locked up, someone in here will
die every seventy-two hours." His gaze didn't miss a
single individual.

Pandemonium broke out. The judge pounded his
gavel, trying to restore order. Police officers rushed
forward to subdue Erickson and haul him away. But
the sound of his threats echoed loudly in Margo's ears.

CHAPTER ONE

LAMAR "STRIKER" JENNINGS walked into the hospital room, stopped and then frowned. "What the hell is he doing working from bed?"

"I asked myself the same thing when I got his call for us to come here," Striker's friend Quasar Patterson said, sitting lazily in a chair with his long legs stretched out in front of him.

"And you might as well take a seat like he told us to do," another friend, Stonewall Courson, suggested, while pointing to an empty chair. "Evidently it will take more than a bullet to slow down Roland."

Roland Summers, CEO of Summers Security Firm, lay in the hospital bed, staring at them. Had it been just last week that the man had been fighting for his life after foiling an attempted carjacking?

"You still look like shit, Roland. Shouldn't you be trying to get some rest instead of calling a meeting?" Striker asked, sliding his tall frame into the chair. He didn't like seeing Roland this way. They'd been friends a long time, and he couldn't ever recall the man being sick. Not even with a cold. Well, at least he was alive. That damn bullet could have taken him out and Striker didn't want to think about that.

"You guys have been keeping up with the news?" Roland asked in a strained voice, interrupting Striker's thoughts.

"We're aware of what's going on, if that's what you want to know," Stonewall answered. "Nobody took Murphy Erickson's threat seriously."

Roland made an attempt to nod his head. "And now?"

"And now people are panicking. Phones at the office have been ringing off the hook. I'm sure every protective security service in town is booked solid. Everyone in the courtroom that day is either in hiding or seeking protection, and with good reason," Quasar piped in to say. "The judge, clerk reporter and bailiff are all dead. All three were gunned down within seventy-two hours of each other."

"The FBI is working closely with local law enforcement, and they figure it's the work of the same assassin," Striker added. "I heard they anticipate he'll go after someone on the jury next."

"Which is why I called the three of you here. There was a woman on the jury who I want protected. It's personal."

"Personal?" Striker asked, lifting a brow. He knew Roland dated off and on, but he'd never been serious with anyone. He was always quick to say that his wife, Becca, had been his one and only love.

"Yes, personal. She's a family member."

The room got quiet. That statement was even more baffling since, as far as the three of them knew, Roland didn't have any family...at least not anymore. They were all aware of his history. He'd been a cop, who'd discovered some of his fellow officers on the take. Before he could blow the whistle he'd been framed and sent to prison for fifteen years. Becca had refused to accept his fate and worked hard to get him a new trial. He served three years before finally leaving prison, but not before the dirty cops murdered Roland's wife. All the cops involved had eventually been brought to justice and charged with the death of Becca Summers, in addition to other crimes.

"You said she's family?" Striker asked, looking confused.

"Yes, although I say that loosely since we've never officially met. I know who she is, but she doesn't know I even exist." Roland then closed his eyes, and Striker knew he had to be in pain.

"Man, you need to rest," Quasar spoke up. "You can cover this with us another time."

Roland's eyes flashed back open. "No, we need to talk now. I need one of you protecting her right away."

Nobody said anything for a minute and then Striker asked, "What relation is she to you, man?"

"My niece. To make a long story short, years ago my mom got involved with a married man. He broke things off when his wife found out about the affair but not before I was conceived. I always knew the identity of my father. I also knew about his other two, older sons, although they didn't know about me. I guess you can say I was the old man's secret.

"One day after I'd left for college, I got a call from

my mother letting me know the old man was dead but he'd left me something in his will."

Striker didn't say anything, thinking that at least Roland's old man had done right by him in the end. To this day, his own poor excuse of a father hadn't even acknowledged his existence. "That's when your two brothers found out about you?" he asked.

"Yes. Their mother found out about me, as well. She turned out to be a real bitch. Even tried blocking what Connelly had left for me in the will. But she couldn't. The old man evidently had anticipated her making such a move and made sure the will was ironclad. He gave me enough to finish college without taking out student loans with a little left over."

"Good for him," Quasar said. "What about your brothers? How did they react to finding out about you?"

"The eldest acted like a dickhead," Roland said without pause. "The other one's reaction was just the opposite. His name was Murdock and he reached out to me afterward. I would hear from him from time to time. He would call to see how I was doing."

Roland didn't say anything for a minute, his face showing he was struggling with strong emotions. "Murdock is the one who gave Becca the money to hire a private investigator to reopen my case. I never got the chance to thank him."

"Why?" Quasar asked.

Roland drew in a deep breath and then said, "Murdock and his wife were killed weeks before my new trial began."

"How did they die?"

"House fire. Fire department claimed faulty wiring. I never believed it but couldn't prove otherwise. Luckily their ten-year-old daughter wasn't home at the time. She'd been attending a sleepover at one of her friends' houses."

"You think those dirty cops took them out, too?" Stonewall asked.

"Yes. While I could link Becca's death to those corrupt cops, there wasn't enough evidence to connect Murdock's and his wife's deaths."

Stonewall nodded. "What happened to the little girl after that?"

"She was raised by the other brother. Since the old lady had died by then, he became her guardian." Roland paused a minute and then added, "He came to see me this morning."

"Who? Your brother? The dickhead?" Quasar asked with a snort.

"Yes," Roland said, and it was obvious he was trying not to grin. "When he walked in here it shocked the hell out of me. Unlike Murdock, he never reached out to me, and I think he even resented Murdock for doing so."

"So what the fuck was his reason for showing up here today?" Stonewall asked. "He'd heard you'd gotten shot and wanted to show some brotherly concern?" It was apparent by Stonewall's tone he didn't believe that was the case.

"Umm, let me guess," Quasar then said languidly. "He had a change of heart, especially now that his niece's life is in danger. Now he wants your help. I assume this is the same niece you want protected."

"Yes, to both. He'd heard I'd gotten shot and claimed he was concerned. Although he's not as much of a dickhead as before, I sensed a little resentment is still there. But not because I'm his father's bastard—a part of me believes he's gotten over that."

"What, then?" Striker asked.

"I think he blames me for Murdock's death. He didn't come out and say that, but he did let me know he was aware of the money Murdock gave Becca to get me a new trial and that he has similar suspicions regarding the cause of their deaths. That's why, when he became his niece's guardian, he sent her out of the country to attend an all-girls school with tight security in London for a few years. He didn't bring her back to the States until after those bad cops were sent to jail."

"So the reason he showed up today was because he thought sending you on a guilt trip would be the only way to get you to protect your niece?" Striker asked angrily. Although Roland had tried hiding it, Striker could clearly see the pain etched in his face whenever he spoke.

"Evidently. I guess it didn't occur to him that making sure she is protected is something I'd want to do. I owe Murdock, although I don't owe Frazier Connelly a damn thing."

"Frazier Connelly?" Quasar said, sitting up straight in his chair. "*The* Frazier Connelly of Connelly Enterprises?"

"One and the same."

Nobody said anything for a while. Then Striker asked, "Your niece—what's her name?"

"Margo. Margo Connelly."

"And she doesn't know anything about you?" Stonewall asked. "Are you still the family's well-kept secret?"

Roland nodded. "Frazier confirmed that today, and I prefer things to stay that way. If I could, I would protect her. I can't, so I need one of you to do it for me. Hopefully, it won't be long before the assassin that Erickson hired is apprehended."

Striker eased out of his chair. Roland, of all people, knew that, in addition to working together, he, Quasar and Stonewall were the best of friends. They looked out for each other and watched each other's back. And if needed they would cover Roland's back, as well. Roland was more than just their employer—he was their close friend, mentor and the voice of reason, even when they really didn't want one. "Stonewall is handling things at the office in your absence, and Quasar is already working a case. That leaves me. Don't worry about a thing, Roland. I've got it covered. Consider it done."

MARGO CONNELLY STARED up at her uncle. "A bodyguard? Do you really think that's necessary, Uncle Frazier? I understand extra policemen are patrolling the streets."

"That's not good enough. Why should I trust a bunch of police officers?"

"Why shouldn't you?" she countered, not for the first time wondering what her uncle had against cops.

"I have my reasons, but this isn't about me—this is about you and your safety. I refuse to have you placed in any danger. What's the big deal? You've had a bodyguard before."

Yes, she'd had one before. Right after her parents' deaths, when her uncle had become her guardian. He had shipped her off to London for three years. She'd reckoned he'd been trying to figure out what he, a devout bachelor, was to do with a ten-year-old. When she returned to the United States, Apollo remained her bodyguard. When she turned fourteen, she fought hard for a little personal freedom. But she'd always known the chauffeurs Uncle Frazier hired could do more than drive her to and from school. More than once she'd seen the guns they carried.

"Yes, but that was then and this is now, Uncle Frazier. I can look after myself."

"Haven't you been keeping up with the news?" he snapped. "Three people are dead. All three were in that courtroom with you. Erickson is making sure his threat is carried out."

"And more than likely whoever is committing these murders will be caught before there can be another shooting. I understand the three were killed while they were away from home. I have enough paperwork to catch up on here for a while. I didn't even leave my house today."

"You don't think a paid assassin will find you here? Alone? You either get on board with having a bodyguard or you move back home. It's well secured there."

Margo drew in a deep breath. Back home was the

Connelly estate. Yes, it was secure, with its state-of-the-art surveillance system. While growing up, she'd thought of the ten-acre property, surrounded by a tall wrought iron fence and cameras watching her every move, as a prison. Now she couldn't stand the thought of staying there for any long period of time...especially if Liz was still in residence.

Margo's forty-five-year-old uncle had never married and claimed he had his reasons for never wanting to. But that didn't keep him from occasionally having a live-in mistress under his roof. His most recent was Liz Tillman and, as far as Margo was concerned, the woman was a *gold digger.*

"It's final. A bodyguard will be here around the clock to protect you until this madness is over."

Margo didn't say anything. She wondered if at any time it had crossed her uncle's mind that they were at her house, not his, and she was no longer a child but a twenty-six-year-old woman. In a way she knew she should appreciate his concern, but she refused to let anyone order her around.

He was wrong in assuming she hadn't been keeping up with the news. Just because she was trying to maintain a level head didn't mean a part of her wasn't a little worried.

She frowned as she glanced up at him. The last thing she wanted was for him to worry needlessly about her. "I'll give this bodyguard a try...but he better be forewarned not to get underfoot. I have a lot of work to do." She wasn't finished yet. "And another thing, Uncle Frazier," she said, crossing her arms over her chest. "I think you forget sometimes that I'm twenty-six and live on my own. Just because I'm going along with you on this, I hope you don't think you can start bulldozing your way with me."

He glowered at her. "You're stubborn like your father."

She smiled. "I'll take that as a compliment." Dropping her hands, she moved back toward the sofa and sat down, grabbing a magazine off the coffee table to flip through. "So, when do we hire this bodyguard?"

"He's been hired. In fact, I expect him to arrive in a few minutes."

Margo's head jerked up. "What?"

Find out what happens when Margo and Striker come face-to-face in FORGED IN DESIRE by New York Times *bestselling author Brenda Jackson. Available February 2017 from Brenda Jackson and HQN Books.*

COMING NEXT MONTH FROM

⬢ HARLEQUIN®

Desire

Available April 4, 2017

#2509 THE TEN-DAY BABY TAKEOVER
Billionaires and Babies • by Karen Booth
When Sarah Daltry barges into billionaire Aiden Langford's office with his secret baby, she strikes a deal—help him out for ten days as the nanny and he'll help with her new business. Love isn't part of the deal...

#2510 EXPECTING THE BILLIONAIRE'S BABY
Texas Cattleman's Club: Blackmail • by Andrea Laurence
Thirteen years after their breakup, Deacon Chase and Cecelia Morgan meet again...and now he's her billionaire boss! But while Deacon unravels the secrets between them, Cecelia discovers she has a little surprise in store for him, as well...

#2511 PRIDE AND PREGNANCY
by Sarah M. Anderson
Secretly wealthy FBI agent Tom Yellow Bird always puts the job first. But whisking sexy Caroline away to his luxury cabin is above and beyond. And when they end up in bed—and expecting!—it could compromise the most important case of his career...

#2512 HIS EX'S WELL-KEPT SECRET
The Ballantyne Brothers • by Joss Wood
Their weekend in Milan led to a child, but after an accident, rich jeweler Jaeger Ballantyne can't remember any of it! Now Piper Mills is back in his life, asking for his help, and once again he can't resist her...

#2513 THE MAGNATE'S MAIL-ORDER BRIDE
The McNeill Magnates • by Joanne Rock
When a Manhattan billionaire sets his sights on ballerina Sofia Koslov for a marriage of convenience to cover up an expensive family scandal, will she gain the freedom she's always craved, or will it cost her everything?

#2514 A BEAUTY FOR THE BILLIONAIRE
Accidental Heirs • by Elizabeth Bevarly
Hogan has inherited a fortune! He's gone from mechanic to billionaire overnight and can afford to win back the socialite who once broke his heart. So he hires his ex's favorite chef, Chloe, to lure her in, but soon he's falling for the wrong woman...

HDCNM0317

*Desperate to escape her sheltered life, Hayley Thompson
quits her job as church secretary to become personal
assistant to bad-tempered, reclusive, way-too-sexy
Jonathan Bear. But his kiss is more temptation than
she bargained for!*

Read on for a sneak peek at
SEDUCE ME, COWBOY
the latest in Maisey Yates's New York Times *bestselling*
COPPER RIDGE series!

This was a mistake. Jonathan Bear was absolutely certain
of it. But he had earned millions making mistakes, so
what was one more? Nobody else had responded to his
ad.

Except for this pale, strange little creature who looked
barely twenty and wore the outfit of an eighty-year-old
woman.

She was… Well, she wasn't the kind of formidable
woman who could stand up to the rigors of working with
him.

His sister, Rebecca, would say—with absolutely no
tact at all—that he sucked as a boss. And maybe she was
right, but he didn't really care. He was busy, and right
now he hated most of what he was busy with.

There was irony in that, he knew. He had worked
hard all his life. He had built everything he had, brick by

brick. And every brick built a stronger wall against all the things he had left behind. Poverty, uncertainty, the lack of respect.

Finally, Jonathan Bear, that poor Indian kid who wasn't worth anything to anyone, bastard son of the biggest bastard in town, had his house on the side of the mountain and more money than he would ever be able to spend.

And he was bored out of his mind.

Boredom, it turned out, worked him into a hell of a temper. He had a feeling Hayley Thompson wasn't strong enough to stand up to that. But he expected to go through a few assistants before he found one who could handle it. She might as well be number one.

"You've got the job," he said. "You can start tomorrow."

Her eyes widened, and he noticed they were a strange shade of blue. Gray in some lights, shot through with a dark, velvet navy that reminded him of the ocean before a storm. It made him wonder if there was some hidden strength there.

They would both find out.

Don't miss
SEDUCE ME, COWBOY
by New York Times *bestselling author Maisey Yates,*
available November 2016 wherever
Harlequin® Desire books and ebooks are sold.

www.Harlequin.com

REQUEST YOUR FREE BOOKS!
2 FREE NOVELS PLUS 2 FREE GIFTS!

H HARLEQUIN®

Desire

ALWAYS POWERFUL, PASSIONATE AND PROVOCATIVE

YES! Please send me 2 FREE Harlequin® Desire novels and my 2 FREE gifts (gifts are worth about $10). After receiving them, if I don't wish to receive any more books, I can return the shipping statement marked "cancel." If I don't cancel, I will receive 6 brand-new novels every month and be billed just $4.55 per book in the U.S. or $5.24 per book in Canada. That's a savings of at least 13% off the cover price! It's quite a bargain! Shipping and handling is just 50¢ per book in the U.S. and 75¢ per book in Canada.* I understand that accepting the 2 free books and gifts places me under no obligation to buy anything. I can always return a shipment and cancel at any time. Even if I never buy another book, the two free books and gifts are mine to keep forever.

225/326 HDN GH2P

Name	(PLEASE PRINT)

Address		Apt. #

City	State/Prov.	Zip/Postal Code

Signature (if under 18, a parent or guardian must sign)

Mail to the **Reader Service:**

IN U.S.A.: P.O. Box 1867, Buffalo, NY 14240-1867
IN CANADA: P.O. Box 609, Fort Erie, Ontario L2A 5X3

Want to try two free books from another line?
Call 1-800-873-8635 or visit www.ReaderService.com.

* Terms and prices subject to change without notice. Prices do not include applicable taxes. Sales tax applicable in N.Y. Canadian residents will be charged applicable taxes. Offer not valid in Quebec. This offer is limited to one order per household. Not valid for current subscribers to Harlequin Desire books. All orders subject to credit approval. Credit or debit balances in a customer's account(s) may be offset by any other outstanding balance owed by or to the customer. Please allow 4 to 6 weeks for delivery. Offer available while quantities last.

Your Privacy—The Reader Service is committed to protecting your privacy. Our Privacy Policy is available online at www.ReaderService.com or upon request from the Reader Service.

We make a portion of our mailing list available to reputable third parties that offer products we believe may interest you. If you prefer that we not exchange your name with third parties, or if you wish to clarify or modify your communication preferences, please visit us at www.ReaderService.com/consumerchoice or write to us at Reader Service Preference Service, P.O. Box 9062, Buffalo, NY 14240-9062. Include your complete name and address.

HD15

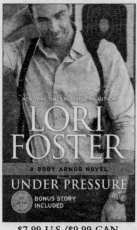